feed

feed

M. T. Anderson

CANDLEWICK PRESS

Thanks to my editors, Liz Bicknell and Kara LaReau,
who helped immensely in the shaping of this book.

o   o   o

Copyright © 2002 by M. T. Anderson

First paperback edition in this format 2012

Excerpt from "Anthem for St. Cecilia's Day" by W. H. Auden from
W. H. Auden Collected Poems edited by Edward Mendelson. Copyright
1945 by W. H. Auden © 1976 by Edward Mendelson, William Meredith,
and Monroe K. Spears, executors of the Estate of W. H. Auden. Reprinted
by permission of Random House, Inc., and Curtis Brown, Ltd.

The Library of Congress has cataloged the hardcover edition as follows:

Anderson, Matthew T.
Feed / by M. T. Anderson. — 1st ed.
p.   cm.
Summary: In a future where most people have computer
implants in their heads to control their environment, a boy
meets an unusual girl who is in serious trouble.
ISBN 978-0-7636-1726-4 (hardcover)
[1. Science fiction.]   I. Title.
PZ7.A54395 Fe 2002
[Fic] — dc21   2002023738

ISBN 978-0-7636-2259-6 (first paperback edition)
ISBN 978-0-7636-6262-2 (second paperback edition)

12 13 14 15 16 17 BVG 10 9 8 7 6 5 4 3 2

Printed in Berryville, VA, U.S.A.

This book was typeset in Berkeley.

Candlewick Press
99 Dover Street
Somerville, Massachusetts 02144

visit us at www.candlewick.com

To all those who resist the feed
—M. T. A.

o   o   o

"O dear white children casual as birds,
 Playing among the ruined languages,
 So small beside their large confusing words,
 So gay against the greater silences
 Of dreadful things you did . . ."

> —from "Anthem for St. Cecilia's Day,"
>   W. H. Auden

Contents

Part 1

moon

1

Part 2

eden

41

Part 3

utopia

73

Part 4

slumberland

205

Part 1

moon

your face
is not
an organ

We went to the moon to have fun, but the moon turned out to completely suck.

We went on a Friday, because there was shit-all to do at home. It was the beginning of spring break. Everything at home was boring. Link Arwaker was like, "I'm so null," and Marty was all, "I'm null too, unit," but I mean we were all pretty null, because for the last like hour we'd been playing with three uninsulated wires that were coming out of the wall. We were trying to ride shocks off them. So Marty told us that there was this fun place for lo-grav on the moon. Lo-grav can be kind of stupid, but this was supposed to be good. It was called the Ricochet Lounge. We thought we'd go for a few days with some of the girls and stay at a hotel there and go dancing.

We flew up and our feeds were burbling all sorts of things about where to stay and what to eat. It sounded pretty fun, and at first there were lots of pictures of dancing and people with romper-gills and metal wings, and I was like, *This will be big, really big,* but then I guess I wasn't so skip when we were flying over the surface of the moon itself, because the moon was just like it always is, after your first few times there, when you get over being like, *Whoa, unit! The moon! The goddamn moon!* and instead there's just the rockiness, and the suckiness, and the craters all being full of old broken shit, like domes nobody's using anymore and wrappers and claws.

The thing I hate about space is that you can feel how old and empty it is. I don't know if the others felt like I felt, about space? But I think they did, because they all got louder. They all pointed more, and squeezed close to Link's window.

You need the noise of your friends, in space.

I feel real sorry for people who have to travel by themselves. In space, that must suck. When you're going places with other people, with this big group, everyone is leaning toward each other, and people are laughing and they're chatting, and things are great, and it's just like in a commercial for jeans, or something with nougat.

To make some noise, Link started to move his seat up and back to whack Marty's knees. I was like trying to sleep for the last few minutes of the flight because there was nothing to see except broken things in space, and when we're going hard I get real sleepy real easy, and I didn't want to be null for the unettes on the moon, at the hotel, if any of them were youch.

I guess if I'm honest? Then I was hoping to meet someone on the moon. Maybe part of it was the loneliness of the craters, but I was feeling like it was maybe time to hook up with someone again, because it had been a couple months. At parties, I was starting to get real lonely, even when there were other people around me, and it's worse when you leave. Then there's that silence when you're driving home alone in the upcar and there's nothing but the feed telling you, *This is the music you heard. This is the music you missed. This is what is new. Listen.* And it would be good to have someone to download with. It would be good to have someone in the upcar with you, flying home with the lights underneath you, and the green faces of mothers that you can see halfway through the windows of dropping vans.

As we flew across the surface of the moon, I couldn't sleep. Link was playing with the seat like an asshole. He was moving it forward and backward. Marty had dropped his bird, these fake birds that were the big spit and lots of people had them, and Marty's bird was floating off, because there was hardly any gravity, and whenever he leaned out to get his bird, Link would slam his seat back like meg hard and it would go bam on Marty's face, and they would start laughing. Marty would be all, "Unit! Just wait one—" and Link would be, "Go for it. Try! Try it!" and Marty would be like, "Unit! You are so—!" And then they would be all big laughing and I felt like a complete bonesprocket for trying to sleep when there was fun. I kept hoping the waitress lady would say something and make them shut up for a minute, but as soon as we got out of Earth's gravitational zone she had gone all gaga over the duty-free.

I didn't want to be sleepy and like all stupid, but I had been drinking pretty hard the night before and had been in mal and I was feeling kind of like shit. So it was not a good way to start this whole trip to the moon, with the seat thumping on Marty's face, and him going, "Unit! I'm trying to get my bird!"

Link was saying, "Go for it."

Marty went, "Linkwhacker! Shit! You're like doing all this meg damage to my knees and my face!"

"Kiss the chair. Pucker up."

They both started laughing again. "Okay," said Marty. "Okay, just tell me which of my frickin' organs you're going to smash this time."

"Keep your tray in the upright position."

"Like what organ? Just tell me."

"Those aren't organs."

"What do you mean?"

"Your face is not an organ."

"My face is too an organ. It's alive."

"Omigod, is there enough oxygen?" said our friend Calista. "Because are you having some kind of neuron death?"

"I'm trying to sleep," Loga complained. She yawned. "I'm flat-lining. Meg."

Then there was this *wham* and Marty was all, "Oh, shit," holding on to his face, and I sat up and was like completely there was no hope of sleeping with these morons doing rumpus on my armrest.

The waitress came by and Link stopped and smiled at her and she was like, *What a nice young man.* That was because he purchased like a slop-bucket of cologne from the duty-free.

impact

So I was tired and pissy from the get-go.

When we got off the ship, our feeds were going fugue with all the banners. The hotels were jumping on each other, and there was bumff from like the casinos and mud slides and the gift shops and places where you could rent extra arms. I was trying to talk to Link, but I couldn't because I was getting bannered so hard, and I kept blinking and trying to walk forward with my carry-on. I can't hardly remember any of it. I just remember that everything in the banners looked goldy and sparkling, but as we walked down to the luggage, all the air vents were streaked with black.

The whole time was like that. The moon went on and on. It was me and Marty and Link and Calista and Loga and Quendy. The three girls had one room at the hotel, and the three of us boys had another room. There were a lot of people there for the break, and kids were all leaping up and down the halls and making their voices echo. It was a pretty crummy hotel, and there weren't enough sheets, and there was hardly any gravity, and no one had a fake ID so they put a lock on the minibar. I was like, "This is a crummy hotel," but Marty was all, "Unit, this is where I stayed last time. It's like meg cheap, and all the staff are made from a crystalline substance."

Our feeds were clear again from all the moon banners, so for a long time we all watched the football game while the girls, they did something else on the feed. They were chatting each other and we couldn't hear them, but they kept laughing and touching each other's faces. I wanted to go to sleep, but every time I tried, *bam!* Link and Marty would suddenly go all fission on me, saying, "Titus! Did you fuckin' see that? Did you see Hemmacher?" I tried to tell myself that being here was not re: sleeping but re: being with your friends and doing great stuff. I tried to concentrate on all the stimulus, and the fun, all of it.

There was not always too good fun, though. We ordered some fancy nutrient IVs from room service but they gave us all headaches, and we went out to this place that Marty said served the

9

best electrolyte chunkies but it had closed a year before. It was dinnertime, so we had dinner at a J. P. Barnigan's Family Extravaganza, which was pretty good, and just like the one at home. We got some potato skins for appetizers. It was at least good to get out of the hotel, because most of the rest of the city had pretty good artificial gravity, so if you dropped things, at least they fuckin' fell. It was almost like normal, which is how I like it.

Then we went back to the hotel. There were parties there, but it was mostly college kids. Usually we can get in, because me and Link and Marty and Calista, we can turn on the charm. Calista is blond and she can do this sorority-girl ice-princess thing, which she does with her voice and her shoulder blades, which makes people think she's older than she is and really important. Link is tall and butt-ugly and really rich, that kind of old rich that's like radiation, so that it's always going *deet deet deet deet* in invisible waves and people are suddenly like, "Unit! Hey! Unit!" and they want to be guys with him. Marty, his thing is that he's good at like anything, any game, and I just stand there silent and act cool, and we're this trio, the three of us guys, being like, total guys, which usually makes people let us in and give us beer.

That didn't work this time. We tried to get in

and we were standing in the doorway and they were all, "Who the hell are you?"

We looked at ourselves. We all looked kind of bad. We looked tired and sleepy, and even though we're all pretty good-looking, except Link, we were all pale and our hair was greasy. We had the lesions that people were getting, and ours right then were kind of red and wet-looking. Link had a lesion on his jaw, and I had lesions on my arm and on my side. Quendy had a lesion on her forehead. In the lights of the hallway you could see them real good. There are different kinds of lesions, I mean, there are lesions and lesions, but somehow our lesions, in this case, seemed like kid stuff.

Later after some showers we went to the Ricochet Lounge. It was very lo-grav/no-grav, and it was all about whamming one person into another in big stuffed suits. The place had been hip, like, a year and a half ago. The slogan was "Slam the Ones You Love!" Now the place just looked old and sad. The walls were all marked up from people hitting them.

Even with his impact helmet on, Link stood out. He's much taller than anyone else, because he's part of a secret patriotic experiment. In the low gravity, his arms seemed like they were everywhere. He swung them around and spun. I was being a little careful when I ran into other people, because of the arm lesion. It had broke open and it was oozing. Still, it was pretty fun at first, launching ourselves off the walls and going like *vvvvvvvvvvvvv* and hitting other people and wrestling while floating to the floor.

I was watching Loga real close. She and I had gone out about six months before, until we had this big argument. Then it was this big thing. She was like, *I never want to see you again,* and I was like, *Fine. Okay? Fine. Then get some special goggles.* But now we were friends, which was good. I think it's always really limp, when guys can't talk to girls they went out with. Plus, I was thinking that maybe Loga and I could hook up again, if we didn't find anyone else, like on the moon or whatev.

I didn't have a thing for Calista or Quendy or even completely a thing (anymore) for Loga. But I was watching Link slamming into them, and when he slammed, it said that he and the girls all knew what each other's bodies would be like, and that was part of the game.

I was unhappy because Loga and I had been a diad, and now when I ran into her at high speeds it wasn't anything like when Link ran into her at high speeds. I thought she and I should have a little secret way of collision. But usually we sailed right past each other.

Marty, who can do anything good, he was off

in a corner doing these gymnastics in midair. He had a ball and he was somehow kicking it in a circle so it came back to his foot. Link said, "Over here," and Marty popped the ball to him, and he kicked it to me.

For a while we played a game with the ball, and we were twirling all over the place, and we were like, what it's called when you skim really close over the surface of something, we were that to the floor, with our arms out, but of course Marty started winning all the time, and Link, who doesn't like to lose, was like, "This is null. This sucks."

"Pass," said Marty. "What's fuckin' doing?"

"That this place sucks," said Link.

Marty said, "Give it a chance, unit."

But Link was like, "No. Play by yourself. Play with yourself," and suddenly everything seemed really stupid.

And then I saw someone watching. I wasn't glad. I looked again.

She was the most beautiful girl, like, ever.

She was watching our stupidity.

There was a valve that led into the food bar. She was in the valve. She had her crash helmet under her arm. She had this short blond hair. Her face, it was like, I don't know, it was beautiful. It just, it wasn't the way—I guess it wasn't just the way it looked like, but also how she was standing. With her arm. I just stared at her. I was getting some meg feed on the food bar and the pot stickers were really cheap.

I stood there wondering what it was that made her so beautiful. She was looking at us like we were shit.

Her spine. Maybe it was her spine. Maybe it wasn't her face. Her spine was, I didn't know the word. Her spine was like . . . ?

The feed suggested "supple."

o   o   o

. . . *attracted to its powerful T44 fermion lift with*
vertical rise of fifty feet per second—and if
you like comfort, quality, and class, the
supple upholstery and ergonomically designed
dash will leave you something like hysterical.
But the best thing about it is the financing—
at 18.9% A.P.R. . . .

o   o   o

. . . ONLY ON SPORTS-VOX — TAKE A MAN, TAKE A GAS
SLED, TAKE A CHLORINE STORM ON JUPITER — AND
BOYS, IT'S TIME TO SPIT INTO THE WIND WITH
ALEX NEETHAM, THE HARDEST, HIPPEST,
HYPEST . . .

o   o   o

. . . *month's summer styles, and the word on the*
street is "squeaky." . . .

o   o   o

. . . *their hit single "Bad Me, Bad You":*
"I like you so bad
And you like me so bad.
We are so bad

It would be bad
If we did not get together, baby,
Bad baby,
Bad, bad baby.
Meg bad." . . .

☉   ☉   ☉

. . . *Hostess M's American Family Restaurants.*
Where time seems to stop while you chew.®

○   ○   ○

Juice

I followed her when I could.

She was sitting in the snack bar now, with her back to the valve. She was all clipped into the seat so she wouldn't float away if she jerked. I bought a snack. It was chocolate mousse in a tube. I hung on to the counter with one hand.

I watched her through my underarm. She was sitting there, with her slamsuit off now and in a bundle. Her helmet was on a hook next to her. I took a slug of tube mousse. I looked back over at her.

She was wearing a dress of gray wool. It wasn't plastic, and the light didn't reflect off it. Wool. Gray wool. Black stockings.

Her shoulders were like, all bent in, as if she didn't want anyone to be looking at her. She was just sitting, clipped in.

The others came through the valve behind me. I kept my head low. I didn't want them to be like, *Hey, unit, hey, hey, Titus, what's doin?* and then she'd look at me. She would be disturbed. Luckily, they came in and immediately Link and Marty started doing these gymnastics, and they got in trouble, so I could stay watching her without them being a mob on me. This guy, he was from the club, he was yelling at them because they kept bouncing in the snack bar, which was off-bounds for still bouncing.

Behind the girl in gray was a big window and you could see we were in a bubble way high up over the moon. Down on the ground, tourists were riding big proteins across the craters. All the stars were out.

The guy was still yelling at the others over by the valve. He was all, *da da da be removed from the premises, da da da, express instructions, da da.*

I lowered my head, and turned it toward the girl in gray.

When she thought no one was looking, she opened her mouth. Something trembled there. Juice. She had filled her mouth with juice.

Da da da, liability, da da da, think you're doing.

I shifted. I watched the juice. For her own amusement, she was letting it go, gentle and sexy.

She just opened her mouth and pushed it out with her tongue. The juice came out of her lips as if it was being extracted real careful by a rock-star dentist who she loved. Her eyes were barely

18

open, and it came out in lo-grav/no-grav as a beautiful purple wobble.

It hung in front of her, her juice. It stayed inches from her face. Her tongue was close behind it, perched in the air like a pink slug gargoyle.

With her eyes almost shut, she watched traces on the drink's round surface swirl.

the nose grid

Link whispered at my side, "This so big sucks."

"This place doesn't suck," said Marty. "It's good."

"Maybe," said Calista, "if there were certain people who didn't go jumping on people's heads near the snack bar, if there weren't those people, then maybe we wouldn't all be standing here having a big shame banquet."

Marty was getting angry that everyone was like turding on his recommendation, and I just wanted them all to shut up somehow, I mean nicely, because suddenly I realized that we didn't really sound too smart. If someone overheard us, like that girl, they might think we were dumb.

I was playing with the magnets on my boots and trying not to look at her. I didn't want her to feel my eyes before I made my move. I was careful. Quendy and Loga went off to the bathroom because hairstyles had changed.

Marty drifted around and made slit-eyes at Link. Link and I were chatting about the girl, like I was going, *She is meg youch,* and he was going, *What the hell's she wearing?,* and I was going, *Wool. It's wool. Like from an animal,* and then Calista did her own chat to us, which was, *If you want to hear about an animal, what about two guys staring with their mouths wide open so they look completely Cro-Magnon?*

That shut us up, and we stared out the window. Wrappers were turning through space like birds.

Quendy came back from the bathroom and said, "Omigod! Like big thanks to everyone for not telling me that my lesion is like meg completely spreading."

"Hon," said Calista, "it's not spreading."

"Omigod! It is going to be like larger than my whole head! I am going to need a hat just to have all this lesion. It will like go onto the brim."

"Exercise the breath," said Link. "Nobody cares about a stupid lesion."

"How can you not?" said Quendy. "It's huge, and it's right on my forehead. It's like *bonnnng!*" She trembled her hands around the lesion like it was a kind of lesion gong.

Loga went, "No one will notice."

"If they don't know you," Marty said, "they're not going to know what you normally look like."

"Oh, so they think that usually my like forehead is like weeping?"

"Ask her," said Link. He pointed to the girl in gray.

He said, "Miss, I wonder if you would, could you look at this girl and tell me if you notice anything?"

The girl turned around and looked at Quendy. She said, "The lesion isn't bad."

Quendy's hands were out in a *please*. "You saw it! See? Like, how far is the air lock?"

"Hon," said Calista. "Listen to the girl."

The girl said, "I've been thinking, because of my neck."

The girl's lesion was beautiful. It was like a necklace. A red choker.

"The face," said the girl, "is a grid. The two big imaginary lines are one down the center of the face and one just across the top of the cheeks. This is my theory, anyway. The nose is where those lines intersect. The more a lesion interferes with those lines, the more noticeable it is. See, the hardest lesion to carry off is one on the nose itself. In your case, you have this lesion which is entirely on the edge of this one quadrant. That's not going to matter. It's not on a line." She unclipped herself and reached up with both her hands and touched her thumbs together, and made football goalposts around Quendy's face. "Framing. See?

Your lesion, it's on the *edge* of your face, so it *frames* your face. It draws attention to your face. The good grid. See, you have this great grid. I'm probably saying way too much."

We were all kind of stunned.

"Yeah," said Calista, sounding confused. "She's right. It just frames your face."

The girl in gray touched her own lesion with a napkin. She said, "I want mine to go all the way around. I want it to be like a necklace, but right now, it's just a torque."

We were all just kind of staring at her like she was an alien. She smiled. We kept staring at her.

"There are times you just want to sink through the floor," she said, "but then you realize there's no air out there."

"Hey," said Marty. "I got a lesion on my foot. You want to see it?"

She smiled sweetly. "No, not really," she said.

Link pointed at his face and was like, "Hey, what about my lesion? Look at this puppy. It bleeds sometimes. You like this?"

She smirked. "Oh, mmm-hm," she said. "You put the 'supper' back in 'suppuration.'"

Link thought that was hilarious. Of course, he didn't have any idea what the hell she was talking about either, but he started laughing while the rest of us were still looking up "suppuration" on the feed English-to-English wordbook.

She was now completely youch on all of our meters, except with the girls, who I could tell had started to chat each other like some ants after someone's buried a missionary alive in the middle of their hill. On the one hand, I thought she was the most amazing person I had ever seen in my life, even if she was weird as shit. On the other hand, I was pretty disappointed she was skeezing this sexy talk with Link Arwaker, who women for some reason always go for, in spite of the fact that he's a meg asshole to them, for example a slurpy question about, "Oh, what about *my* lesion? Let's talk more about *me* and *my* open sores."

Marty was trying to make up lost ground by saying, "Maybe you could change the bandages on my foot," but that was clearly just disgusting to everyone. We were all like, "Unit, no one wants to see your damn foot," and, "Jesus, Marty unit, stow the mess-hole."

Link was asking her, "Who are you? Where do you come from?"

And then she looked at me. Just at me, and I knew she was wondering what I thought about the guys and seductiveness and skeeze and all. She was waiting for me to say something, to see if I was going to skeeze like Marty and Link. I wondered whether she wanted me to skeeze. She seemed really smart from what she said, and she was pretty, and I was still thinking about that globe of juice floating in front of her face. I was still thinking about the beauty of how that juice had been born delicately from her lips, how it had been born whole, and how her tongue stood there afterward to see the juice make its trembling progress into the world.

But I had nothing to say.

She and the girls spent the rest of the hour fixing Quendy's hair to like showcase the lesion. Usually, Quendy is just like a kind of broken, little economy model of Calista, and she knows that, and feels real bad about it. But when this girl helped her, it wasn't like that. Quendy was the center of everyone for a long time.

That was why I kept looking at the girl in gray, and started to want, more than anything else that night, to be with her.

o o o

. . . based on the true story of a clone fighting to save her own liver from the cruel and ruthless original who's farming her for organs.

"Nature . . . vs. Nurture." A Primus prime-time feedcast event.

Image of a girl weeping on a courtroom floor. *"I am not Girl Number Two! Please, Judge Spandex! I'm also Number One! I'm not a product, but a person!"*

Image of a girl holding a blaster to a twin's temple. *"Remember, bitch. You can't spell 'danger' without DNA."*

Blam.

o o o

. . . the cola with the refreshing taste of citrus and butter . . .

o o o

. . . an adventure in slouching . . .

Calculon. New solutions for . . .

*. . . It's dance. It's dance, dance, dance. That's fun.
    Fun's fun, and fun's what you can have.
    There's nothing to stop you from fun. Do you
    see the bodies? Can you smell the beat? Then
    you'll come and roar with us. Come and
    throw your boots at superstars. Come thrash
    in the cool until your head opens up, and you
    see the veins of the people you love bright as
    branches against the sky, and burnt in your
    brain will be the fun, all of the fun, and the
    lights, and the Doppler fade of screaming you
    heard at the Rumble Spot. The Rumble Spot.*

*The Rumble Spot: an ocean of chaos in the Sea of
    Tranquillity.*

Images of Coke falling in rivulets down chiseled
mountainsides; children being held toward the
sun; blades slicing grass; a hand, a hand extended
toward the lemonade like God's at Creation; boys
in Gap tees shot from a rocket; more lining up

with tin helmets; Nike grav-gear plunging into Montana; a choir of Jamaican girls dressed in pinafores and strap-on solar cells; dry cleaners ironing the cheek prostheses of the rich; friends clutching at birds made of alloys; law partners jumping fences; snow; altitude; tears; hugs; night.

o o o

the moon
is in the
house of boring

She was on the moon all alone. Here it was, spring break, and she was on the moon, where there was all this meg action, and she was there without friends. She said she just walked through the crowds and watched, and she saw all these great things that way. She said she was there to observe.

There were crowds in the domes at night, spraying Gatorade from hoses, and all these college guys without shirts lifting their arms. There was a beetle that walked through the lanes and gave out prizes, which seemed really good, but she said that really, the prizes, they were kind of shitty when you looked at them close-up, because sometimes parts weren't included. She saw pools filled with foam.

Her name was Violet.

We asked her to come with us. We wanted to go to sleep by then, but we were on the moon, even if it sucked, and it was spring break, you know, with the action, so there was no way we were admitting we wanted to go to sleep. We told her we were thinking about going to some club called the Rumble Spot that we'd heard about on the feed.

"I don't know," she said.

But I was like, "You got to go. You can go and, you know, observe."

Marty said, "It will be a, a, you know, fuckin', it will . . ." He kind of wiggled his hand.

"Since you put it that way," she said, kind of fresh. Calista laughed. Suddenly I knew Calista was either going to love her or hate her.

After we were walking for a few minutes, it was, on the scale, maybe closer to hate, because Marty and Link and I were all walking around Violet and asking her all these questions, and she was asking us stuff, and we were telling her, and I don't think the other girls really were too skip about walking behind us.

Link said he wanted to get cranked before we went, and he said was there any place where we could drink without IDs? Marty said he knew of this one place, which was called Sombrero Dot, and he went there before with his cousin. He said it wasn't too out-of-the-way.

We got there and it had been torn down. They had built a pretty nice stucco mall there, so Loga and Quendy said we should go in and buy some cool stuff to go out in. That seemed good to us. I wanted to buy some things but I didn't know what they were. After we walked around for a while, everything seemed kind of sad and boring so we couldn't tell anymore what we wanted. Our feeds tried to help, and as we were walking around we were getting all the prices of things, but really the only thing that I wanted to get was a pair of infrared knee bands, and I could get better ones off the feed, and have them sent to my house, than in the stupid physical moon stores. Quendy bought some shoes, but the minute she walked out of the store she didn't like them anymore. Marty couldn't think of anything he wanted, so he ordered this really null shirt. He said it was so null it was like ordering nothing.

Now it was even later and we wanted to go to the club, but we hadn't got drunk yet, so Link said maybe we could take a cab to the hotel and break into the minibar.

As we were driving through the tube streets, there was all of this commotion because of the protests about the moon. There were all these kids, what my dad calls Eurotrash, and they were standing in the middle of the square and broadcasting to everyone all these slogans, and it was hard not to receive, because they were so angry, but the cab drove right by them, and they didn't stop us. They were protesting all these things, some of them even were protesting the feed. They were like shouting, "Chip in my head? I'm better off dead! Chip in my head? I'm better off dead!" Loga rolled her eyes and was like, "Omigod."

We got back to the hotel. Kids were running down the halls with their fake birds. The fake birds were still in style. It was stupid, because the birds didn't even fly or sing or anything.

We went to the girls' bedroom and started to assault the minibar. I wanted to break it open quickly, because Violet was looking like she wasn't having fun. She was sitting all stiff on the bed.

"Just a sec," I said.

She nodded, but it was kind of polite.

Calista was whispering to Link, "What's her problem?"

We tried the minibar first with a comb, then with kicking. We threw it against the wall, which wasn't as hard to do with almost no gravity.

"You broke off a . . . a thing," said Marty. "You broke off a fuckin' thing."

"A caster," I said.

"Caster," said Link, pointing at my nose. "Good one."

You know your break sucks when the most

brag part of the night is you coming up with the word "caster."

Violet was just sitting on the bed, playing with her thumb. Her shoulders were droopy and her feet were turned in. In fact, all the girls looked kind of on suspend. Calista and Loga were staring into space, watching something on the feed.

"Fuck," said Link, kicking the minibar. "I want to get weasel-faced."

"There's no way you're getting weasel-faced," I said. "Let's just go."

Marty was like, "We could malfunction."

"Oh, god," said Loga and Quendy, rolling their eyes.

Violet looked real uncomfortable now. It was pretty obvious she really didn't want to be with us.

Link looked around at the girls' faces. "What's the problem?" he said.

"Drop it, Link," I said. "We're not going in mal."

"I heard about this great site called Lobe-reamer. Eighty-five bucks, one click, and we'll be completely raked for an hour and a half. We won't know which way's up. That's big, big scrambled, for cheap."

"Unit!" said Marty. "We're fuckin' there!"

Link said, "Okay. Let's . . ."

"Drop it, units," I said. "No one wants to be fuguing."

"Am I no one?" said Link.

Calista was like, "Are you asking in terms of sex appeal?"

"Ow!" Marty said.

Link said, "Shut up, Marty."

Calista chatted all of us guys, *Don't like push this. Especially because the girl is meg un-into it.*

Link was like, *Lobe-reamer. Lobe-reamer! Do those words mean nothing to you?*

Brake, Link. Brake and upgrade.

There was no way he was getting lobotomized or weasel-faced, so we just went over to the Rumble Spot unslammed. It was their Youth in Action night, so we could get in.

It was meg big big loud. There was everything there. There was about a million people it seemed, and lights, and the beat was rocking the moon. There was a band hung by their arms and their legs from the ceiling, and there was girders and floating units going up and down, and these meg youch latex ripplechicks dancing on the bar, and there were all these frat guys that were wearing these, unit, they were fuckin' brag, they were wearing these tachyon shorts so you couldn't barely look at them, which were $789.99 according to the feed, and they were on sale for like $699 at the Zone, and could be shipped to the hotel for an additional $78.95, and that was just one great thing that people were wearing. When I looked around, I wanted so much, that all of the prices were coming into my brain, and it was *bam bam bam,* like fugue-joy, and Loga and Quendy and Calista were already out on the dance floor, and my feed was like going fried, going things about the dance and pictures they were feedflinging across the dance floor of people on fire doing the moves.

Violet was screaming to me. I couldn't hear a thing. She was like, *"Da da da? Da da!"*

I was like, "What?"

She chatted me, *This is a scene.*

I was like, *Don't you dance?*

Not really. Are these all college kids?

I bet most of them. Look at the guy in the, you know, that thing? The neck bat?

Bow tie.

Bow tie.

He was maybe a hundred or so, dancing with the ripplechicks, a man in a dirty old tweed jacket, and he had this long white hair that looked kind of yellow, and his eyes were wide, like he was in mal, but I'm not sure he was in mal. He kept on sticking his thumbs up in the air.

And then they turned off the artificial gravity and we all went bounding accidentally, and it was like people cruising past each other with their necks kinked, and Violet grabbed on to my arm, and now I was thinking that even though she looked really uncomfortable, and like she was watching some kind of bugs in an experiment, it wasn't so bad being a bug as long as she grabbed on to my arm, so I said, *Don't worry. We'll drift down.*

Sorry, she chatted.

No wrong, I said.

Really. I didn't mean to grab you.

No wrong.

I put my hand over her hand on my arm, and then she smiled and took her hand out from under my hand, and by that time we'd come down again, and were bending our knees.

The guy with the tweed jacket had on a jetbelt, and he was flying around near the ceiling.

You don't look like you're having fun, I chatted to her.

I will.

When?

I'm not used to this.

What do you do for fun?

When?

Normally.

I haven't been on the moon before.

I mean, anywhere. What do you do?

The man with the bow tie was standing near

us. He was trying to talk to Link by cranking Link's head around and shouting into his ear. Link was backing away.

Are you *having a good time?* she asked.

The moon really isn't working out, I said.

Next time, maybe you should try Mars.

Yeah, I've been to Mars, I said. *It was dumb.*

Suddenly, she laughed. *Are you serious?*

Yeah, I'm serious.

Omigod, she said. *Mars is a whole* planet.

And it's dumb!

She was like, *Dumb?*

She was starting to piss me off.

I said, *Yes, dumb.*

The whole world?

Dumb.

The whole world.

Dumb.

Oh, this is golden.

The Red Planet was a piece of shit.

I don't believe you could — but I couldn't receive any more of her chat because our feeds were spiking, and the music was getting louder, with the band singing "I'll Sex You In," and I saw her folding her arms like she didn't like me, and I didn't like her, and everyone was pulsing, even the old guy, and everyone was hopping, and they were scatterfeeding pictures across the floor: tribal dances, stuff with gourds, salsa, houses under breaking dams, women grinning, women oiling men with their fingertips, women taking out their teeth, girls' stomachs, boys' calves, rockets from old "movies" flaring, bikini tops, fingers creeping into nostrils, silos, suns—and the old man was standing by our side, and trying to yell, but we couldn't hear him, so he leaned closer, and said to us, to Marty and Violet and now Link and me, he said, yelled, more like, he yelled: "We enter a time of calamity!"

We stared.

"We enter a time of calamity!"

We tried to back up, all of us except Violet, who was confused, and Link was saying, "This unit, he's like completely fuguing. He has this—"

"We enter a time of calamity! We enter a time of calamity!"

The old man reached out and, with a metal handle, touched me on the neck.

Suddenly, I could feel myself broadcasting. I was broadcasting across the scatterfeed, going, helplessly, *We enter a time of calamity! We enter a time of calamity!* I couldn't stop.

And he had touched Violet now, and Link, and Marty, and from all of them, it was coming, *We enter a time of calamity! We enter a time of calamity!*

And now I could feel that it was coming from other places, too, other people he had touched, and Marty was trying to say that he'd never had this before, it was kind of cool, but he couldn't because his signal was jammed just with that, over and over again, all of us in a chorus, going, *We enter a time of calamity! We enter a time of calamity!* and people were turning toward us. People were looking. We were standing in a line and the old guy was standing in front of us. People were moving away. The police were coming. I could see them. I couldn't really move much.

I felt a kind of kicking in my face and I discovered it was my mouth, which was saying the time of calamity thing, but at the top of my lungs. We were shouting, we were broadcasting, and then over us all, as the cops came through the crowd, the guy started this crazy calling, both out loud and on the feed, this crazy calling over it all, over our chorus, and it went:

"*We enter a time of calamity. Blood on the tarmac. Fingers in the juicer. Towers of air frozen in the lunar wastes. Models dead on the runways, with their legs facing backward. Children with smiles that can't be undone. Chicken shall rot in the aisles. See the pillars fall.*"

While we said, again and again, "*We enter a time of calamity. We enter a time of calamity,*" and others in the room said it, too, and Violet looked as scared as me, and I tried to take her hand, and she tried to take mine, and the police were by our side, hitting the man over the head again and again with stunners and sticks, and he fell on one knee, and finally my fingers found her wrist, Violet's. It felt so soft, like something I had never felt before. It felt like the neck of a swan in the wind.

And then the police were at our sides, whispering to us, "We're going to have to shut you off now. We're going to have to shut you off."

And then they touched us, and bodies fell, and there was nothing else.

Part 2

eden

awake

The first thing I felt was no credit.

I tried to touch my credit, but there was nothing there.

It felt like I was in a little room.

My body—I was in a bed, on top of my arm, which was asleep, but I didn't know where. I couldn't find the Lunar GPS to tell me.

Someone had left a message in my head, which I found, and then kept finding everywhere I went, which said that there was no transmission signal, that I was currently disconnected from feednet. I tried to chat Link and then Marty, but nothing, there was no transmission signal, I was currently disconnected from feednet, of course, and I was starting to get scared, so I tried to chat my parents, I tried to chat them on Earth, but there was no transmission etc., I was currently etc.

So I opened my eyes.

college try

"Nothing," she said.

I had gotten up and was sitting on a chair beside her. We were in a hospital. We took up a ward.

Link was still asleep. Nurses went by.

I said, "I can't see anything. Through the feed."

"No," she said. "Or through my hospital gown. So stop trying."

I smiled. "You know, I thought maybe . . ."

"Sure you did. Want some apple juice?"

We'd been up for fifteen or twenty minutes. Everything in my head was quiet. It was fucked.

"What do we do?" she asked.

I didn't know.

boring

There was nothing there but the walls. We looked at them, and at each other. We looked really squelch. Our hair and stuff. We had remote relays attached to us to watch our blood and our brains.

There were five walls, because the room was irregular. One of them had a picture of a boat on it. The boat was on a pond or maybe lake. I couldn't find anything interesting about that picture at all. There was nothing that was about to happen or had just happened.

I couldn't figure out even the littlest reason to paint a picture like that.

still boring

Our parents had been notified while we were asleep. Only Loga hadn't been touched by the hacker. She hadn't let him touch her, because he looked really creepy to her, so she stood way far away. There were also others, people we'd never met, who had been touched, and they were in the wards, too. He had touched thirteen people in all.

There was a police officer there, waiting in a chair. He told us that we would be off-line for a while, until they could see what had been done, and check for viruses, and decrypt the feed history to get information to use against the guy in court. They said that they had identified him, and that he was a hacker and a naysayer of the worst kind.

We were frightened, and kept touching our heads. Suddenly, our heads felt real empty.

At least in the hospital they had better gravity than the hotel.

missing the feed

I missed the feed.

I don't know when they first had feeds. Like maybe, fifty or a hundred years ago. Before that, they had to use their hands and their eyes. Computers were all outside the body. They carried them around outside of them, in their hands, like if you carried your lungs in a briefcase and opened it to breathe.

People were really excited when they first came out with feeds. It was all *da da da, this big educational thing, da da da, your child will have the advantage, encyclopedias at their fingertips, closer than their fingertips, etc.* That's one of the great things about the feed—that you can be supersmart without ever working. Everyone is supersmart now. You can look things up automatic, like science and history, like if you want to know which battles of the Civil War George Washington fought in and shit.

It's more now, it's not so much about the educational stuff but more regarding the fact that everything that goes on, goes on on the feed. All of the feedcasts and the instant news, that's on there, so there's all the entertainment I was missing without a feed, like the girls were all missing their favorite feedcast, this show called *Oh? Wow! Thing!,* which has all these kids like us who do stuff but get all pouty, which is what the girls go crazy for, the poutiness.

But the braggest thing about the feed, the thing that made it really big, is that it knows everything you want and hope for, sometimes before you even know what those things are. It can tell you how to get them, and help you make buying decisions that are hard. Everything we think and feel is taken in by the corporations, mainly by data ones like Feedlink and OnFeed and American Feedware, and they make a special profile, one that's keyed just to you, and then they give it to their branch companies, or other companies buy them, and they can get to know what it is we need, so all you have to do is want something and there's a chance it will be yours.

Of course, everyone is like, *da da da, evil corporations, oh they're so bad,* we all say that, and we all know they control everything. I mean, it's not great, because who knows what evil shit they're up to. Everyone feels bad about that. But they're the only way to get all this stuff, and it's no good getting pissy about it, because they're still going to control everything whether you like it or not. Plus, they keep like everyone in the world employed, so it's not like we could do without them. And it's really great to know everything about everything whenever we want, to have it just like, in our brain, just sitting there.

In fact, the thing that made me pissy was when they couldn't help me at all, so I was just lying there, and couldn't play any of the games on the feed, and couldn't chat anyone, and I couldn't do a fuckin' thing except look at that stupid boat painting, which was even worse, because now I saw that there was no one on the boat, which was even more stupid, and was kind of how I felt, that the sails were up, and the rudder was, well, whatever rudders are, but there was no one on board to look at the horizon.

cache & carry

I had a few pages cached, from right before the feed stopped. I flipped through them sadly. I went back and forth between them. One was a message from the crazy asshole, which said, *You have been hacked by the Coalition of Pity.* The other was a good sale at Weatherbee & Crotch, which, by this time, I had probably missed. It was too bad, because I would have liked to have been able to take the opportunity to check out these great bargains, for example they had a trim-shirt with side pockets that I thought I probably would have bought, except it only came in sand, persimmon, and vetch.

night, and boring

It was Saturday night. The main lights were out. It had been a day since any of us had heard from the feed. Our parents were probably already on the moon, and were coming to the hospital the next morning.

For most of the day since we woke up after the attack, we had stared at the walls. We'd been sitting in our beds, and we tapped our feet on the rails. None of us could get the tune of "I'll Sex You In" out of our heads. Someone kept starting it up, and then the others would swear and tell them to shut up. Then we couldn't help ourselves, and we'd start to tap it out on our trays with a spork.

Link had finally woken up, and he paced up and down the floor. Loga came by during the afternoon and she talked to all of us, and she kept saying, "Ohhhhh! Ohhhhh!" in this sorry tone of voice, which was nice, except that then she would pause and we could tell she was m-chatting all the news back to our friends on Earth. Occasionally, she'd forget and she'd say out loud to no one, "Omigod! Yes! Right here!" or "Hello . . . ?" or whatever it was she was saying in her head. She would laugh at jokes we couldn't hear.

Once, she went to the bathroom, casual-like, and came back with her hair parted a different place. Calista and Quendy watched her.

Later, without saying anything, they went and did theirs different like that, too.

Marty was sometimes saying his usual kind of thing, which was like, "Fuck this shit. Fuck this." He wanted to be out playing basketball or something.

There was nothing to do. Violet stared at her hands in her lap. I looked over at her. I smiled, you know, supportive. She looked at me and then went back to staring at her hands.

Now it was night, and all the big lights were out. We were lying there. There were machines that were taking our pulse and shit. We were all supposed to be sleeping.

I heard Violet walk across the floor and head for the bathroom. A few minutes later, I heard her walking back.

"Hey," I said.

"Yeah. Hey," she said. She stopped.

"You can . . . ," I said. I pulled myself up against the pillows. "Why don't you sit down for a sec?"

She sat down in the chair by my bed. I could see the curve of her nose against my pulse, which was green and bumpy.

We sat there for a little while. I was thinking, *This is nice. We're just sitting here. We don't have to say anything.*

I felt real contented. I lay my head back on my pillow.

I looked over at her face. I could see the light from my heartbeat on her tears.

I said. "You're . . . hey. You're crying."

"Yes," she said.

"You don't . . ." I didn't know how to say what I wanted. I tried, "You don't seem like a crier."

"No," she said.

We sat. Now the silence wasn't very good. Her head was low. I could see the curve of her cheek against my brain waves, which were red and loopy.

She said, "You go try to have fun like a normal person, a normal person with a real life — just for one night you want to live, and suddenly you're screwed."

"You're not screwed."

"I'm screwed."

We sat there. I wanted to say something to

cheer her up. I had a feeling that cheering her up might be a lot of work. I was thinking of how sometimes, trying to say the right thing to people, it's like some kind of brain surgery, and you have to tweak exactly the right part of the lobe. Except with talking, it's more like brain surgery with old, rusted skewers and things, maybe like those things you use to eat lobster, but brown. And you have to get exactly the right place, and you're touching around in the brain, but the patient, she keeps jumping and saying, "Ow." Thinking of it like this, I started to not want to say anything. I kept thinking of nice things I could say, like, "I'm glad you went out last night, because that's how I met you," or, "And I think you *are* a normal person," but they all seemed just smarm.

So we just sat there, together, and we didn't say anything. And it wasn't bad.

I hoped she could see my smile in the light of my brain.

father

When my father got there the next morning, he didn't stay long. He was being very powerful and businesslike. He was dressed up, and he looked like he was ready to give some orders and sort things out. He looked like everyone around us was stupid and he was going to roll up his sleeves and do some real clarity work.

He stood there staring at me for a few seconds, and I was like, "What? *What?*"

He seemed surprised, and then blinked. He said, "Oh. Shit. Yeah, I forgot. No m-chat. Just talking."

I was like, "Do you have to remind me? What's doing? How's Smell Factor?"

"Your brother has a name."

"How's Mom?"

"She's like, whoa, she's like so stressed out. This is . . . Dude," he said. "Dude, this is some way bad shit."

I could completely feel Violet watching us. She was listening. I didn't want to have her judging us, and thinking we were too boring or stupid or something.

My father asked me to tell him what happened. I told him, leaving out some parts, like trying to break in to the minibar. He just kept shaking his head and going, "Yeah," "Yeah," "Yeah," "Oh, yeah," "Yeah," "Shit," "Yeah."

Finally, he stood up. I could tell he was pissed. He held up his hands. He said, "They want to subpoena your memories. This is this thing which is . . . Okay, this is bullshit."

After a minute, he said to someone who wasn't there, "Okay. Okay." He turned to me and said, "I'm going down to the police."

"Dad?" I said. "When am I going home?"

Dad put his hand over his ear. "Okay," he said. His mouth twitched. He nodded to someone.

He hit me on the knee and left.

I was staring at the wall and the stupid boat picture.

I heard Quendy say to Violet, "When are your parents coming?"

She said in a flat voice, "They're busy."

"Busy?"

"Yeah. With jobs. I guess they can't come at all."

salad days,
w/sneeze guard

The next morning, we hadn't heard anything. We decided we needed to be cheered up big-time.

So Marty invented this game where we blew hypodermic needletips through tubing at a skinless anatomy man on the wall. We spat the needles and tried to pin his nads.

It was the beginning of a great day, one of the greatest days of my life. We all played the dart game, and we laughed and sang "I'll Sex You In." Everyone was smiling, and it was skip.

The surprise was, Violet was the best at the dart game. She always won. I sucked.

She tried to teach me. It was a complete turn-on. She took my hand and put the tube in my mouth.

She whispered, "Aspirate. With the tongue."

People were really impressed. Link and Marty were completely hitting on Violet for it, but she didn't pay them any attention, and sometimes she would stand there with one hand on my shoulder. I could feel that she was putting pressure on it, and that she didn't need to stand with all her weight because I was there.

Then Loga came in to the hospital for a while, and we were all talking to her about stuff when she stopped for a second because the girls' favorite feedcast, *Oh? Wow! Thing!,* was on. They were all like, "Tell us what's happening, tell us what's happening," so we all gathered around her in our little gowns, and she sat there cross-legged on the bed and told us, "Okay, so like now Greg's walking in, and he's . . . omigod, he's completely malfunctioning—he's completely in mal, and Steph is crying on the sofa. Okay, so she goes . . ." And she told us the story of what was happening as it happened, and we all sat there, smiling. I never heard Loga tell a story this good before, and she even used her hands and stuff, and her eyes were vacant like she was seeing some other world, which I guess she was. "Jackie is sitting on the front of the boat? And he holds his hand up, and he's going . . . he's going . . . omigod, he goes, 'Organelle, I always loved you from when we first went sailing.'"

Quendy was like, "Oh, god! This is so romantic!"

"Oh, meg. Big meg. You can feel the breeze on

your skin. It's warm, like those nights, you know, when we're like—we're like, 'We're always going to be young.' The breeze is like that. I wish you could feel it." We all shivered. She said, "You can smell the salt. The moon's out. It's high above everything, and soft."

Quendy actually cried one tear.

Violet and I looked at each other. We didn't look away.

We still were like that, looking into each other's eyes and all, when the doctor came in and was like, *What the hell had happened in the examination room, what's with all the needles?* and he was upgrading to homicidal and going all, *Da da da professional care unit, da da da dangerous and costly da da infection da da da,* etc. Luckily, Link's mom heard him yelling at us, and she's a complete dragon, so she gave him a piece of her mind. She told him that we were all suffering from a very stressful experience and we weren't used to these kinds of stresses and he had to understand that we had to have our fun, too. I still felt kind of bad about it, because we made a big mess, and Violet was completely meg blushing, but at least we didn't get like shoved into orbit on cybergurneys or something.

I liked being just a few beds away from her. We could wave. We all talked about old music, like from when we were little, and all the stupid bands they had back then, and the stupid fashions we liked in middle school, like the year when the big fashion from L.A. and shit was that everyone wanted to dress like they were in an elderly convalescent home, there was this weird nostalgic chic for that, so we all remembered having stretch pants and velour tops, and Calista had even bought one of those stupid accessory walkers at Weatherbee & Crotch. There were those stupid ads for having your pants pulled up like around your chest. Violet said she still had a cane at home.

When we were eating dinner, sitting on her bed side by side, she said to me, "This is fun."

"It weirdly is," I said.

"Maybe these are our salad days."

"Huh?"

"You know. Happy."

"What's happy about a salad?"

She shrugged. "Ranch," she said.

the garden

Violet was off someplace talking to the doctor. I say "someplace" because we were using the examination room to blow needles at the anatomical guy's basket.

Link and Calista were standing real close by the vibrating bath, and I realized that they had probably decided to hook up. It looked like Calista was getting over Link being so stupid, which was brag, because he's a nice guy. Quendy sat there on the table, glaring at them.

Violet came back from the doctor. She was all intense looking. I asked what was wrong. She said she'd found a place she wanted to show me. I said sure, and I went with her. We went out into the hall. The shouting from the examination room was more distant. We walked for a ways through some tubes and so on. People floated by automatically on gurneys.

She walked in front of me. Her slippers went *fitik, fitik, sliss, fitik* on the floors. They were soft sounds, like the sounds mouths make when they open and close. I watched her from behind. When we stopped to wait for an uptube, she lifted her ankle so her heel came out of the slipper, and with her toes she slid it back and forth on the tiles without thinking about it. She massaged the floor. When the uptube was free, she settled her foot back in, and walked, *fitik, fitik, sliss, fitik,* right on in.

She took me up to a huge window. We stood in front of it. Outside the window, there had been a garden, like, I guess you could call it a courtyard or terrarium? But a long time ago the glass ceiling over the terrarium had cracked, and so everything was dead, and there was moon dust all over everything out there. Everything was gray.

Also, something was leaking air and heat out in the garden, lots of waste air, and the air was rocketing off into space through the hole, so all of the dead vines in the garden were standing straight up, slapping back and forth, pulled toward the crack in the ceiling where we could see the stars.

"Whoa," I said.

"Isn't it beautiful?"

"It's like . . . ," I said. "It's like a squid in love with the sky."

She was only looking at me, which was nice. I hadn't felt anything like that for a long time.

She rubbed my head, and she went, "You're the only one of them that uses metaphor."

She was staring at me, and I was staring at her, and I moved toward her, and we kissed. The vines beat against each other out in the gray, dead garden, they were all writhing against the spine of the Milky Way on its edge, and for the first time, I felt her spine, too, each knuckle of it, with my fingers, while the air leaked and the plants whacked each other near the silent stars.

dead language

We were watching Marty invent a game called Struggle of the Dying Warrior. It involved him being tied with all of his limbs, like his arms and his legs, onto the frame of his bed with the rubber tubing. Then he tried to get up and walk. He was not getting very far.

Violet and I were sitting on a bunk, swinging our legs in rhythm. We were talking about our families. I told her that I had a little brother. She said I hadn't mentioned him. I said he was a lot younger and a real pain.

Violet asked me about my mom and dad. I told her that my dad did some kind of banking thing, and my mom was in design. I didn't understand what my dad did exactly. Whatever it was, he was off doing it on the moon until tomorrow, when they were going to tell us about our feeds.

When I asked her what her dad did, she

said, "He's a college professor. He teaches the dead languages."

"People study that?"

She shrugged. "I guess."

"Okay. So what are the dead languages?"

"They're languages that were once important but that nobody uses anymore. They haven't been used for a long time, except by historians."

"Like what languages?"

"You know, FORTRAN. BASIC."

"What does one sound like?"

She slid off the bunk, and went to get her bag. She opened it and pulled out something, which was a pen. She also had paper.

I looked at her funny. "You write?" I said. "With a pen?"

"Sure," she said, a little embarrassed. She wrote something down. She put the pad of paper on my lap.

She asked me, "Do you know how to read?"

I nodded. "I can read. A little. I kind of protested it in School™. On the grounds that the silent 'E' is stupid."

"This is the language called BASIC," she said.

On the paper, it said:

```
002110 Goto 013500
013500 Peek 16388, 236
013510 Poke 16389, 236
```

She read it to me. I could tell the numbers fine.

"So what does that mean?" I asked.

"It's the first thing my dad teaches the students on the first day," she said. "It means, 'I came, I saw, I conquered.'"

I looked at her pen. "You write all the time," I said, completely in awe.

"I've done it since I was little."

"Do you write . . . stuff?"

"Not stories or anything. I just write down things I see sometimes."

"On paper."

"Yeah."

I looked at her. "You're one funny enchilada," I said.

She nodded real quiet.

"Doesn't your hand get all cramped up?" I asked. "Don't you end up like, hook-hand?" I made hook-hand. She made hook-hand. We pawed each other with hook-hand.

She shook her head and smiled.

I asked, "Why don't you use the feed? It's way faster."

"I'm pretentious," she said. "Really pretentious."

"Yeah, so the studio audience has noticed, but seriously."

"Seriously."

Suddenly, something occurred to me. I looked up at her.

Marty had fallen to his knees, and was being pulled back toward the bed by the tubing. His cheeks were puffed out. His hands were in fists. His fingers were getting blue. All of the ridges on his arms stood out. Calista and Link were whistling with their fingers in their mouths. The other people in the ward were yelling, "Shut up! Would you all shut up?"

I asked Violet, "Your father, he's a college professor, but he was too busy to come see you after you like completely collapsed from a hacker attack? Too *busy*?"

She looked me in the eye. "No," she said, "but that's what I told you."

release

The salad days couldn't last forever. We really wanted to get back to Earth. Everyone wanted to forget how sucky the moon had been.

Tuesday, just before lunch, a doctor and a policewoman and a technician came in. Our parents were all talking over in the corner. The rest of us were all sitting around, talking about spaceship disasters.

The technician called us all to attention and went through this whole thing, he was sorry for the delay, but they wanted to be absolutely sure there was no permanent hack, that our feeds were safe, etc. He was all like, *da da da, must have been a difficult time for all of us, da da da, we would find our normal service resumed without interruption, da da da da da, he was meg sorry we had to go through this, and he had complied with the police and handed over our data, da da da, like thank you all again for your patience.*

One by one, we went into the examination room.

In there, there were nurses and the doctor and the technician. The nurses were watching the relays, our blood pressure and all. They were like, "Don't worry about anything. You'll feel it all coming back in a few seconds." The doctor touched a bootstick to my head.

He said, "Okay. Could we like get a thingie, a reading on his limbic activity?"

The bootstick was cold on my neck. I could feel the little hairs standing up around it. There was some kind of static electricity.

They moved the bootstick a little. I heard it beep.

"You should feel it now," said one of the nurses.

I didn't feel anything. I looked around. They were watching me closely.

"No," I said. I shifted on the bed. I didn't feel anything. I said, "Nothing. I feel nothing."

"Hold your head still," said the doctor.

He shifted the bootstick and it beeped again.

I kicked my heels against the bed. "There's nothing. Nothing," I said.

"Why don't you—" said the nurse. *Pulse up. Rising.*

Limbic activity okay?

He's just nervous.

Don't worry. It'll hit him in like a second.

We have readings on engram formation.

Signal engaged.

Don't drop the exterior relays yet.

The Ford Laputa. Sky and Suburb Monthly says there's no other upcar like it. And we agree.

"There you go," said the nurse.

You'll be more than a little attracted to its powerful T44 fermion lift with vertical rise of fifty feet per second — and if you like comfort, quality, and class, the supple upholstery and ergonomically designed dash will —

They slapped me on the back. I laughed, and the doctor and I did these big grins. I went back out into the other room, and we were all starting to feel it now. We were all starting to feel it good —

. . . name is Terry Ponk, and I'd like to tell you about upper-body strength . . .

And the feed was pouring in on us now, all of it, all of the feednet, and we could feel all of our favorites, and there were our files, and our m-chatlines. It came down on us like water. It came down like frickin' spring rains, and we were dancing in it.

. . . Celebrate fun. Celebrate friends. You've just come through something difficult, and this is the time for a table full of love and friendship and the exciting entrees you can only find at . . .

We were dancing in it like rain, and we couldn't stop laughing, and we were running our hands across our bodies, feeling them again, and I saw Violet almost hysterical with laughter, rubbing her cheeks, and pulling her hands down across her breasts, her chin up in the air.

. . . big bro? Big bro, you there? Mom says I should . . .

. . . until one crazy day when this cranky old woman and this sick little boy meet a coy-dog with a heart of gold—and they all learn an important lesson about love. The NYT called it . . .

. . . hits a grounder to the mound . . .

. . . In other news, protests continued today against the American annexation of the moon. Several South American countries including Brazil and Argentina have submitted requests to join the Global Alliance in response. President Trumbull spoke from the White House. "What we have today, with the things that are happening in today's society, is . . ."

She held my hand—we found each other's hands through the like, the waterfall, and—

. . . If you liked "I'll Sex You In," you'll love these other popular slump-rock epics by hot new storm 'n' chunder band Beefquake, full of riffs that . . .

. . . We handpicked our spring fashions . . .

and holding hands, we danced.

. . . Hardgore, *the best feed-sim battle game ever to rip up the horizon. Sixty levels of detonation and viscera just waiting to fly at your command, Captain Bastard. If you don't feel slogging waist-deep within fifteen seconds, we'll eat our fucking hats . . .*

. . . *In your absence, you may not have heard* . . . Hand in hand, we danced.

Part 3

utopia

normal

Things were back to normal real quick. We went back to Earth, and we all rested up, and our moms brought us ginger ale in bed. We chatted all the time on the feeds and shared music and shit. We had this major debate going on because we watched the *Oh? Wow! Thing!* and there was this part where Organelle asked Jackie whether she had meg hips and he was like, "Since you ask, we both could work out more," and she was like, "You shithead, you should've lied," and so all the guys were saying, *no way, if she asked him this complete question he should answer it,* and the girls were like, *if you ever insult how I look then you're completely shallow,* and we were like, *but she asked,* and they were like, *omigod, you don't get it,* and Link said if they really didn't want to know how they looked, then how come they asked so much, and then I said this thing, and Calista said this thing, and it was like, *da da da da da, da da da da da, da da da da da,* all day. It was kind of fun. I like debates where you argue about different points of view.

My family, they were coming and going. I saw them on the landings, or sometimes, when I went down to the kitchen, behind the counters. My dad didn't really talk to me except to walk up and check to see if I had a fever, which I didn't, because it was a software problem. My mother was always holding on to my brother, Smell Factor, like squeezing him like a doll. She was real busy with him and she went to peewee league games for him and even took him to work with her sometimes. When she wasn't around in the afternoons, he sat in his closet watching *Top Quark,* with it broadcasting all over the place, so I watched it, too, because there was nothing else to do really but watch *Top Quark* and eat Chipwiches.

Cap'n Top Quark, that whole planet is so sad that I think they'll need a whole lot of good thoughts and hugging!

That's why, lickety-split, and we're on our way. Charm Quark, prepare the Friend Cannon. Boson, turn our biggest, orangest sails toward Cryos, on the planet Sadalia.

Aye, aye, sir! You've made me one happy particle, sir!

Smell Factor had one of those birds now, one

of the ones that didn't fly or sing, the metal ones, so I could tell they were meg yesterday. Stuff always starts with people who are cool and in college, and then works down, until when the six-year-olds get it, it's like, who cares? The birds must have been yesterday for a while, because I didn't see them in any ads, and even Smell Factor was leaving his around and not clutching it.

A few days later, I went out on errands, because really, there was no problem anymore. It felt good to get out and to see all of the upcars in tubes and in the parking lots, just normal stuff, like people walking and talking on their feeds, and kids hanging out and shit. There were all the suburbs stacked on top of each other, like Apple Crest and Fox Hollow, and I would just fly through the tubes in the suburbs in my parents' upcar, looking at all the houses and the lawns, each one in its own pod, and everything was all like neat. Then I'd go home and sit on my bed and watch the feed, and everything seemed normal.

It's times like this that I'm real glad I have friends. They say friends are worth your weight in gold.

We had a party at the end of the week over at Quendy's, because her parents were off choking somewhere. That was when everyone was having those choking parties. I mean, it was completely midlife crisis.

It was the first time I saw Violet since we were on the moon. It was brag because she didn't have a ride, and I could borrow my parents' upcar, so I got to fly over and pick her up. I met her at a mall near her house. The mall was right on the surface, and you could see the sky through the dome. She was waiting there and looking up at the sun hitting one of the department stores.

Violet lived in a suburb that was a few hundred miles away from my suburb, so while we drove we had a little time to talk before we got to the party.

It was great because we had music on our feeds, and it was the same music, so I knew she was hearing the same notes that I was hearing, and our heads were like moving together, and she put her hand near the lift lever, so when I got to the exit tube and went to lift us, her hand was there, and our fingers closed over the lift lever, and we lifted it together, and were flung up into the sky.

We were going along pretty fast, and going around towers and shit, and she asked me, "What'll a party be like?"

"Like a party."

"I haven't been to many."

"You . . ." I shrugged. "You do this . . . I don't know. It's fun. It's a party. What do you do instead of parties?"

"My friends and I are all home-schooled, so

we're a mixed bag. Bettina's mother has us come over and weave ponchos."

"You don't go to School™?"

"Alf's parents teach us how to breechload their antiaircraft gun."

"Whoa. Can you show me?"

"Here's the surprising thing: It's all in the wrists."

"Unit."

"Yeah. Unit. God, I'm so excited to be going to a real party."

"Oh yeah?"

"Will it be like it is on the feed?"

I patted her hand. "Yeah. I mean, dumber, but yeah."

"Why, this makes me feel like a special girl. The specialest girl in the world."

She raised up her hand, and we knocked knuckles together.

She leaned back in her seat. She pulled some seat belt out and then let it roll back in. We were both thoughtful for a minute. There were some weather blimps in front of us. They were all yellow in the sunset that was spreading over the Clouds™. We flew between them. We could barely see the silver of their blimp-hides through the color of syrup. They were like a herd.

She asked, "Do you think things are going to be different?"

"From what?"

"From the way things were before."

I looked at her. She looked serious, suddenly. I shrugged. I said, "It's good to have people again, like all these people, talking to you in your head."

"We've all been through this big thing together," she said. "It's got to change us somehow."

She rested her arm along the back of my seat. I leaned my head back. I could feel my hairs rub against her arm.

Even to my hairs, her arm felt soft.

undervalued truffle

We got to the party and it was a pretty good party, but low-key.

When we got there, for a second we stood in the entryway, because Link and Marty were playing each other at this game, *The Cranky Tumble of Dark House,* one of the ones with zombies and mutants, and they were all spinning around and shooting their fingers like guns. They couldn't see anything, just the gamefeed, so when Violet walked in, Marty almost whacked her in the stomach with his fist. He and Link were swearing and hopping up and down on the marble tiles.

"Unit," said Link. "Just get out of the way."

Marty was like, "Out of the fuckin' way! We're—Oh, shit!—We're—oh . . . Unit!" He was all shouting at Link, who was like missing some shot at a spine-leech.

We went into the living room and over to the table where Quendy had all the drinks and beer. People were sitting around drinking, and some of them had music on their feeds and were sitting around talking to it, and some others had imported a feedcast of *Snowblind,* a comedy about a young man who nothing ever happens to, until one crazy day when he crosses the mob at a ski resort and finds out what's really buried in those moguls—and then all hell breaks loose! (NC-17)

Violet looked kind of timid, now that we were there. She took a deep breath and went over to say hi to Calista. I stood around and talked with Quendy for a few minutes. Quendy was at first really nice and normal, talking about how it was good to see that we were doing okay, and how she was okay, and everything was fine. Then she started this glaring at Calista, and she was chatting me like, *Do you think Calista and Link are doing it?*

I shrugged and was like, *Yeah. I bet.*

He's such a pig. He did it with me like—Oh. Never mind.

Quendy glared at Calista and popped a popcorn shrimp into her mouth from way down below, with her thumb.

She was like, *I'm tired of just being the friendly one who everyone like steps all over.*

Yeah, I chatted. *How do you do that, with the shrimp and your thumb?*

Okay. I'll show you. Hey, are you going out with Violet?

Yeah.

That's great. I think she's meg nice.

Yeah.

Calista says she's kind of stuck-up? But I don't agree at all. Like, Calista's the one who's stuck-up.

Calista said that?

Yeah. You want to try the shrimp on your finger?

She showed me how to pop the shrimp. As she did it, I looked across the room and saw Violet talking to Calista, and both of them were frowning. I was worried that something bad had happened, so I m-chatted her, like, *Hey, beautiful. What's doing?*

Heyyyyy, handsome. Just talking with Calista. Having a nice little chat. I made the mistake of saying we were back to the picayune grind. Now she keeps going, "'Picayune'?!? 'Picayune'?!?" and pretending I'm French. I wish I hadn't said anything.

I looked around me. Everyone was nodding their heads to music, or had their eyes just blank with the feedcast. It was just a party. Nothing but a party.

From one direction, I heard a kid say, "I think the truffle is like completely undervalued."

And from the other direction, a girl was saying, "But he *never* pukes when he chugalugs."

It was like nothing had happened. We were watching feedcasts as if our brains had never been invaded by the asshole. Loga was laughing with her front teeth showing, as if she'd never been different from the rest of us, the one left with the feed when the rest of us didn't have it. Some guy was pouring the beer. Link and Marty were doing like acrobatics in the entryway, fighting invisible demons.

And everything was completely normal.

The truffle was completely undervalued.

o   o   o

*. . . which the President denied in an address early
on Tuesday. "It is not the will of the American
people, the people of this great nation, to
believe the allegations that were made by
these corporate 'watch' organizations, which
are not the majority of the American people, I
repeat not, and aren't its will. It is our duty as
Americans, and as a nation dedicated to
freedom and free commerce, to stand behind
our fellow Americans and not cast . . . things
at them. Stones, for example. The first stone.
By this I mean that we shouldn't think that
there are any truth to the rumors that the
lesions are the result of any activity of
American industry. Of course they are not the
result of anything American industry has
done. The people of the United States know, as
I know, that that is just plain hooey. We need
to remember . . . Okay, we need to remember
that America is the nation of freedom, and
that freedom, my friends, freedom does not
lesions make." The President is expected to
veto the congressional . . .*

o   o   o

the others
in mal

The party went on. I couldn't concentrate anymore. We watched *Snowblind*. The guy in it, he fell off a platform at a mob-owned ski lift and landed in powder next to a sexy assassin with a heart of gold. I was feeling strange sitting next to Violet, and she wasn't laughing, which was weirding me out. She was just sitting there. The feedcast went on and on, and they all went up the mountain on skis and shot at each other and finally they all learned an important lesson about love. Then it was over.

I went upstairs to take a whizz, and Marty and Link were dragging me into a bedroom.

"Unit," Link said. "Unit, you are about to walk through the mirror."

"It is time," Marty said, "for Bulb-tweaker."

"Oh, unit," I was like, "is this malfunction?"

"Hey hey hey hey hey, this is a great site. It's fuckin' smooth as glass."

"'Bulb-tweaker'?"

"It's just a mild scrambler," said Link.

"I can completely see straight," said Marty. He pointed. "That's right in front of me."

There were other guys in there, too, and one girl. They were whispering. Someone had gone completely fugue on the bed.

"Do a burst. Then crank it down to a slow burn."

"Okay," said Marty. "I'm going to go again."

"Unit," said Link, punching me on the arm. "Fly the friendly skies."

I was like, "Not tonight."

"Come on, unit."

"I don't think Violet's into the mal."

"Oh, come on, unit, she'll never know."

"What is this, shitheads?" I said. "Cut the *ABC Afterschool Special*."

"She'll never know!" said Link.

I said, "What did we just go through? Unit?" I whapped myself on the back of the head. "Remember? Like, what did we just . . . ? Huh?"

"Huh?"

"Never mind."

"What?"

"I said never mind."

"Okay," said Link. "Your loss. Here I go. You with, Marty?"

"I'm with."

They spread out their arms and closed their eyes, and you could see when it hit them. They got the shudder first, and then their heads rocked, and they were big stumbling, and they went backward, and there were all these people back there on the bed and a chair and the floor, blinded, doing the quiver. Link's tongue came out. It was purple from candy.

I went out and to the bathroom. When I was done, I went back downstairs. Quendy and Violet were talking. Quendy was like, "Where is everyone?" but I didn't tell her they were up getting scrambled in the master bedroom.

Violet asked if I wanted to walk out in the yard for a minute, and I said sure, so we went out. We were standing on the porch and it was much cooler out there. The dome on the yard's pod was all blue, like it was night, which it was, I mean, up on the surface, but it was blue there at the house, too.

We stood, leaning on the railing. The night was perfect. We shut out the music from the feed. It was funny, then, to look back in and see people moving to nothing.

She said, "You're quiet."

I nodded.

"What's doing?" she asked.

"No real one thing."

We just stood there together.

I said, "You didn't like the feature."

She said, "It was okay."

"You didn't laugh."

"I liked the mountains. All the pine trees. I'd like to go to the mountains. Wouldn't it be nice? With a fire?"

I pictured the mountains and the fire and a snowball fight and let's-get-out-of-these-wet-clothes, and I said, "Yeah. Sure."

"I want to get out to the country," she said. She looked at me. "What's really doing?"

I couldn't tell her about the guys going in mal. I didn't want her looking at them while they were on the wall-to-wall carpeting and doing the quiver. I didn't want her to look at them as if she was sorry.

Finally, I said, "People have just gone so quick back to like before."

"Why?" she said. "What happened?"

I didn't tell her about them upstairs. I just told her about sitting in the living room, and hearing the guy who was like the truffle was under-valued, and the girl who was like he never pukes when he chugalugs. I told her about them and then I looked for the memory of them, which I still had, and I played it for her. She knew exactly what I was talking about.

She went, *Brittle.*

I feel like we're the only two of us who like remember the, like, the thing.

People want to forget.

You can't blame them.

She looked at me. She didn't say anything for a second, and then she said, "My feedware is damaged."

"What? In your—in your brain?"

She put her hand up next to her scalp. "It'll be fine. But I'm the only one who had damage. They're trying to fix it."

"What's wrong? Can you still get like, stuff and shit?"

She laughed. "Yeah. Both of them. I'm fine. But they say they have to find some way to make adjustments. Something happened when the guy hacked. Most people, the hack just jammed them for a while. Somehow it affected mine more. Something's still wrong."

"Holy shit."

"Do you remember one day when we were on the moon, the doctors took me out to talk to me alone? Then I came back and found you, and took you up to the air-loss garden? The doctors, they were talking to me about this. They said that it would probably stabilize. It hasn't yet."

"Holy shit."

"They say it will probably be fine."

"Holy shit."

She patted me on the chest. "Calm," she said. "The rose will bloom ere long."

"Yeah. What-fuckin'-ever." She watched me. I stared at her. I thought about Marty and Link going in mal.

She chatted, *What are you thinking about?*

Nothing.

It can't be nothing.

I thought about Link and Marty's eyes rolled back. And I lied, like, *I'm just wondering whether he meant truffles the mushroom or truffles the candy.*

She laughed and touched my face. I felt like I was protecting her from something and that felt good, like I was a man already. I hugged her like a man and we kissed. For a long time, we stared at each other. I liked the way the synthetic breeze was on her hair. We stood, looking out at the shrubs, and the motorboat up on a trailer, and I felt like I was in love, and our arms were around each other.

She leaned close to my head and took a handful of my hair in her hand and pulled my head down. She whispered, "Keep thinking. You can hear our brains rattling inside us, like the littler Russian dolls."

nudging

That night, the night after the party, I had something that I thought was a dream, with me at a great site where all the games were free and you could play anything. So I was thinking different even about pretty dumb games like *Turbo Checkers*, because if you can get anything for free, what the hell, so I started one of them, which was this fantasy game, and I was putting on some elf gloves, and stringing my bow, when I could feel that someone was nudging my feed. They were nudging it, like with their cheek or nose.

In my dream, I asked them who they were.

In my dream, they told me they were the police. They asked me if I was a victim of the hack at the Rumble Spot.

In my dream, I said yes.

In my dream, they told me okay, go back to sleep.

In my dream, I said who were they really?

They said that they were going to be running some tests on me, and that I should think about something else.

I said that they weren't the police, so who were they really?

They said, here is the lizard you have always been wanting. We took the liberty of giving it a nice new collar.

I asked if all these games were mine.

All yours, they said. All yours. Good night, sweetie. They're all yours. Take them. All yours.

In my dream, I thought they were the hacker group, the Coalition of Pity.

But when I woke up, I didn't remember that for weeks. What I remembered was just the games, which, once I was awake, I couldn't find, and the elf gloves, and the bow, and the lizard that was all mine.

o o o

. . . AMURICA: A PORTRAIT IN GEEZERS . . .

*. . . I remember, as the last forests fell . . . at about
that time, we would see hawks and eagles in
the cities. People walked outside more, back
then. The temperature usually didn't get
above a hundred. There were streets in the
cities, and eagles flew over them, wobbling
without moving their wings.*

*I remember seeing the hawks perched on street
lamps, during those last days of the American
forests. They had come from the mountains,
maybe, or pine woods that were now two or
three levels of suburb, but the hawks sat in
our cities like kings. They would not look
down from their lampposts as thousands of
downcars went by underneath. It was like
they sat alone on Douglas firs.*

*I miss that time. The cities back then, just after the
forests died, were full of wonders, and you'd
stumble on them — these princes of the air on
common rooftops — the rivers that burst
through city streets so they ran like canals —
the rabbits in parking garages — the deer
foaling, nestled in Dumpsters like a Nativity.*

o o o

lose the chemise

It was maybe, okay, maybe it was like two days after the party with the "never pukes when he chugalugs" that Violet chatted me first thing in the morning and said she was working on a brand-new project. I asked her what was the old project, and she was like, did I want to see the new one? I said, *Okay, should I come over to su casa? I've never been there,* and she was like, *No, not yet. Let's meet at the mall.*

I was like, *Okay, sure, fine, whatever swings your string,* and she was all, *Babycakes, you swing my string,* which is a nice thing for someone to say to you, especially before you use mouthwash.

So I flew over to the mall near her house through the rain, which was coming down outside in this really hard way. Everyone had on all their lights until they got above the clouds. Up there it was sunny, and people were flying very businesslike.

The mall was really busy, there were a lot of crowds there. They were buying all this stuff, like the inflatable houses for their kids, and the dog massagers, and the tooth extensions that people were wearing, the white ones which you slid over your real teeth and they made your mouth just like one big single tooth going all the way across.

Violet was standing near the fountain and she had a real low shirt on, to show off her lesion, because the stars of the *Oh? Wow! Thing!* had started to get lesions, so now people were thinking better about lesions, and lesions even looked kind of cool. Violet looked great in her low shirt, and besides that she was smiling, and really excited for her idea.

For a second we said hello and just laughed about all of the stupid things people were buying and then Violet, she pointed out that, regarding legs to stand on, I didn't have very much of one, because I was wheeling around a wheelbarrow full of a giant hot cross bun from Bun in a Barrow.

I said, "Yum, yum, yum."

She was like, "You ready?"

I asked her what the idea was.

She said, "Look around you." I did. It was the mall. She said, "Listen to me." I listened. She said, "I was sitting at the feed doctor's a few days ago, and I started to think about things. Okay. All right. Everything we do gets thrown into a big calculation. Like they're watching us right now. They can tell where you're looking. They want to know what you want."

"It's a mall," I said.

"They're also waiting to make you want things. Everything we've grown up with—the stories on the feed, the games, all of that—it's all streamlining our personalities so we're easier to sell to. I mean, they do these demographic studies that divide everyone up into a few personality types, and then you get ads based on what you're supposedly like. They try to figure out who you are, and to make you conform to one of their types for easy marketing. It's like a spiral: They keep making everything more basic so it will appeal to everyone. And gradually, everyone gets used to everything being basic, so we get less and less varied as people, more simple. So the corps make everything even simpler. And it goes on and on."

This was the kind of thing people talked about a lot, like, parents were going on about how toys were stupid now, when they used to be good, and how everything on the feed had its price, and okay, it might be true, but it's also boring, so I was like, "Yeah. Okay. That's the feed. So what?"

"This is my project."

"Is . . . ?"

She smiled and put her finger inside the collar of my shirt. "Listen," she said. "What I'm doing, what I've been doing over the feed for the last two days, is trying to create a customer profile that's so screwed, no one can market to it. I'm not going to let them catalog me. I'm going to become invisible."

I stared at her for a minute. She ran her finger along the edge of my collar, so her nail touched the skin of my throat. I waited for an explanation. She didn't tell me any more, but she said to come with her, and she grabbed one of the nodules on my shirt — it was one of those nodule shirts — and she led me toward Bebrekker & Karl.

We went into the store, and immediately our feeds were all completely Bebrekker & Karl. We were bannered with all this crazy high-tech fun stuff they sold there. Then a guy walked up to us and said could he help us. I said I didn't know. But Violet was like, "Sure. Do you have those big searchlights? I mean, the really strong ones?"

"Yeah," he said. "We have . . . yeah. We have those." He went over to some rack, and he took these big searchlights off the rack. He showed us some different models. The feeds had specs. They showed us the specs while he talked.

When he went into the back to get another,

cheaper searchlight, I said to Violet, "What next?"

She whispered, "Complicating. Resisting."

Bebrekker & Karl were bannering us big. It was, *We've streamlined the Tesla coil for personal use — you can even wear it in your hair! With these new, da da da,* and *Relax, yawn, and slump! While our greased cybermassage beads travel up and down your back! Guaranteed to make you* etc., like that.

I was like, "Okay, huh?" but the guy came back and he had another searchlight.

He told us, "You can see shit real good with this one? I have one of these on my upcar. It's sometimes like — whoa, really — whoa. There was this one time? And I was flying along at night and I shined the light down at the ground, to look at the tops of all the suburb pods? And all over the top of them, it looked like it was moving, like there was a black goo? So I turned up the brightness, and I went down, and I shined it more bright, and it turned out the black moving goo was all these hordes of cockroaches. There were miles of them, running all over the tops of the domes. They kept on trying to get out of the light, so wherever you shined it, there would be this — "

"I'd like to mount the light on my belly," Violet said. "Would that be possible?"

He looked at her funny. "With a swivel head?"

"Sure. Then I could swivel it."

"What's this for?"

"Something special," she said, in this low voice. She rubbed my arm up and down, sexily.

He was like, "Whoa. I can't even think." He gave me the thumbs-up.

She winked at me. It was kind of a turn-on.

She got him to send her all of the feedstats for the lamp, but then she didn't buy it. She didn't have it mounted. Instead, she thanked him a real lot, and then she took me out of the store, and I was starting to get the picture and think it was all pretty funny.

We kept going from place to place, asking for weird shit we didn't buy. She took me to a rug store, and a store with old chests and pieces of eight and shit, and we went to a toy store and she asked them to explain the world of Bleakazoid action figures, which is a dumbass name if I ever heard one, but they explained it all. It was mainly they were these muscular people from a parallel world, which is usually how it is. We didn't buy anything.

We ran through the big hallway with her tapping her head and saying, "Hear that? The music?" It was pop songs. "They have charts that show which chords are most thumbs-up. Music is marketing. They have lists of key changes that get thirteen-year-old girls screaming. There's no difference between a song and an advertising jingle anymore. Songs are their own jingles. Step lively. Over here."

We went to a clothing store and she held up all these stupid dresses, and the girl there was like, *I'm helping a weird kid, so I'm going to be really fake,* so she kept smiling fake, and nodding really serious at all the dresses Violet held up, and she was all, "That will look great," and Violet said, "I don't know. D'you think? He's pretty wide in the chest."

The girl looked at me, and I was frozen. So I said, "Yeah. I work out."

Violet asked me, "What are you? What's your cup size?"

I shrugged and played along. "Like, nine and a half?" I guessed. "That's my shoe size."

Violet said, "I think he'd like something slinky, kind of silky."

I said, "As long as you can stop me from rubbing myself up against a wall the whole time."

"Okay," said Violet, holding up her hands like she was annoyed. "Okay, the chemise last week was a mistake."

I practically started to laugh snot into my hand.

We went to some more clothing stores, and

we looked at all these dumb sweaters and pretended we liked them, and we looked at makeup that she wouldn't wear, and a gravel-tumbler, and we went to a DVS Pharmacy Superstore, and she comparison-shopped for home endoscopy kits.

We were looking at the endoscopy kits when she started whispering to me, "For the last two days, okay? I've been earmarking all this different stuff as if I want to buy it—you know, a pennywhistle, a barrel of institutional lard, some really cheesy boy-pop, a sarong, an industrial lawn mower, all of this info on male pattern baldness, business stationery, barrettes . . . And I've been looking up house painting for the Antarctic homeowner, and the way people get married in Tonga, and genealogy home pages in the Czech Republic . . . I don't know, it's all out there, waiting."

I picked up one box. "This one is the cheapest. You swallow the pills and they take pictures as they go down."

She said, "Once you start looking at all this stuff, all of these sites, you realize this obscure stuff isn't obscure at all. Each thing is like a whole world. I can't tell you."

"How's your like," I pointed at my head, "how's your feedware working out?"

"It's fine. You're not listening."

"I'm just wondering."

She asked me, "What do you think?"

"I liked the guy in Bebrekker & Karl. I wonder if it's true, about the cockroaches."

"What do you think about resisting?" she asked me really hard. Her jaw muscles were sticking out.

I said, "It sounds great, as long as I get to wear the chemise." She laughed.

We went to dinner at a J. P. Barnigan's Family Extravaganza. We had mozzarella sticks and then I had a big steak. She got a Caesar salad. There were free refills on drinks. Afterward, we were sitting there in the booth, and I asked her whether she wanted a ride home. She said no. I said was she sure, and she said yes.

I said, "What's doing with your parents?"

"What do you mean?"

"Well, with your house, and why you have me meet you here instead. And why didn't your dad come to the moon? When we were, you know."

She looked at me funny. She said, "Do you know how much it costs to fly someone to the moon?"

I guessed. "A lot?"

"Yeah. Yeah, a lot. He wanted to come, but it would have been, like, a month of his salary. He saved up for a year to send me. Then I went, and that stuff happened."

"He saved up for a year for you to go to the moon?"

"Yeah." She said, "Hey, here's what you can do. You can drop me at the feed technician's office. I have an appointment."

We made out for a minute in the car. Then I flew her a few miles away, to a technician. I left her there. Before I pulled out of the tube by his office, I looked back at her, standing by the door. She had her hands on her elbows. She was pinching the elbow skin and pulling it.

She waited there, pinching and pulling, and then went in.

sniffling

That night, I chatted her after I went to bed. I was like, *Violet. Violet?*

She was like, *Hey. Hey there.*

It was great, going to the mall today. I had a good time. I enjoyed that whole thing.

Finally, she was like, *I did, too.*

I could tell something was wrong. It was something about the way she was sending things on the feed.

I asked, *Are you crying?*

There was a long feed silence. I could hear programming.

She was like, *Yeah. Just for practice.*

What's doing?

Never mind, she chatted. *Never mind.*

Didn't you have a real good time?

I wish you were here, she said.

I thought about her lying in bed. Maybe in

some pajamas, so she was warm. I said, *I wish I was there, too.*

Look, she said, changing the whole subject. *Look at everything I got from the feed. It's going crazy with everything we looked at today. It's trying to work for me.*

This perky voice on her feed said, *Hi! I'm Nina, your personal FeedTech shopping assistant! Tired of that gross-out smell in your mouth? Try FreshGorge Glottal Deodorant—your boyf will thank you big-time! Hey, Violet Durn, what a skip kinda day you had! You go shop, girl! Here's some more great info about all the brag stuff you asked about!*

Violet started to forward me things. There were sites for the spotlights and the dresses and the endoscopy kits, and she sent them in flurries. Once they started coming, they started to call others to them, and I could feel them doing that call, and they were all around me. They came to us. It was like they were lots of friendly butter-flies, and we were smeared with something, and they kept coming and coming, and their wings were winking beautifully, and more and more came. And they were landing on our fingers, and on our lips, and on our eyes, opening and closing? And we were going—*Whoa! Whoa! Whoa!*

It was crazy.

a new place

Being with Violet was great.

She hadn't had much of the stuff you see on the feed when she was younger. A lot of it was too expensive, or her father just said no. But she had watched all the shows about how other people live normally, and she really wanted to live like the rest of us. So she and her other home-schooling friends had tried to copy us. For example, he said she couldn't have toy guns, because they were against his beliefs, so she had to pick up anything—pieces of wood or bent metal—and use them like a toy gun, and pretend it was just as good as a real one made of plastic.

I was afraid that she would be too smart for me, but she wasn't. I don't mean she wasn't smarter, because she was, but just that there was so much she hadn't done. She was like a little kid, all excited when I was just meeting her at the mall for the day, and we walked from store to store or went on the air slides or shopped underwater. She had hardly ever done any of it before. She was always new.

We sat in the mall and made up stories about people who passed by. Shoppers walked around us on the concourses, their mouths moving, talking to people who weren't there. They were all muttering.

We made up stories about how they'd given birth to monsters in attics.

We went into stores, and we laughed and laughed.

It was like she took my hand, or I took her hand, and we ducked through doorways, and together we went to an old place, and it was a new place.

We went there holding hands.

the dimples
of delglacey

Okay, but sometimes, though, I did get worried that she was too smart for me.

I don't do too good in School™. We were back in School™, so I was reminded pretty often that I was stupid.

School™ is not so bad now, not like back when my grandparents were kids, when the schools were run by the government, which sounds completely like, Nazi, to have the government running the schools? Back then, it was big boring, and all the kids were meg null, because they didn't learn anything useful, it was all like, *da da da da, this happened in fourteen ninety-two, da da da da, when you mix like, chalk and water, it makes nitroglycerin,* and that kind of shit? And nothing was useful?

Now that School™ is run by the corporations, it's pretty brag, because it teaches us how the world can be used, like mainly how to use our feeds. Also, it's good because that way we know that the big corps are made up of real human beings, and not just jerks out for money, because taking care of children, they care about America's future. It's an investment in tomorrow. When no one was going to pay for the public schools anymore and they were all like filled with guns and drugs and English teachers who were really pimps and stuff, some of the big media congloms got together and gave all this money and bought the schools so that all of them could have computers and pizza for lunch and stuff, which they gave for free, and now we do stuff in classes about how to work technology and how to find bargains and what's the best way to get a job and how to decorate our bedroom.

It was still hard, there were some times when none of us did good, and I felt stupid, and we all felt stupid, and Loga and Calista were like, *Omigod! This is so dumb!*

Could the teacher be any more, please, condescending?

Omigod, I know. Like, thanks for the heapin' helpings of yawn banquet.

And I sat there with my palms pressed into my forehead, thinking about Violet, at home, being smart. I would think about some conversation we were having where I was dumb.

Like she was always reading things about how

everything was dying and there was less air and everything was getting toxic. She told me about how things were getting really bad with some things in South America, but she couldn't really tell exactly how bad, because the news had been asked to be a little more positive. She said that it made her frightened to read all this kind of thing, about how people hated us for what we did. So one time I said to her that she should stop reading it, because it was just depressing, so she was like, *But I want to know what's going on,* so I was like, *Then you should do something about it. It's a free country. You should do something.* She was like, *Nothing's ever going to happen in a two-party system.* She was like, *da da da, nothing's ever going to change, both parties are in the pocket of big business, da da da,* all that? So I was like, *You got to believe in the people, it's a democracy, we can change things.*

She was like, *It's not a democracy.*

I hated it when she got like this, because then she wasn't like herself, I mean, she wasn't like this playful person who drags me around the mall doing crazy shit, she was suddenly like those girls in School™ who sit underground and dress all in black with ribbing and get an iron fixture for their jaws and they're like, "Capitalist fool— propaganda tool," holding up both their hands, etc. When she said things like *It's not a democracy,*

III

suddenly I couldn't stand to be having this whole conversation. I was like, *Oh, yeah,* and she was like, *It's not,* and I was like, *Oh, okay,* and she said, *No, it's not a democracy,* and I was like, *Yes it is,* and she was like, *No it isn't,* and I got sarcastic, so I was like, *No, sure, it's all fascist, isn't it? We're all fascists?*

Then she was like, really gently, *No, please, I'm not trying to be an asshole. It's not a democracy.*

I was like, *Then what is it?*

A republic. It's a republic.

Why?

Because we elect people to vote for us. That's my point.

So why is it like that?

Because if it was a democracy, everybody would have to decide about everything.

I thought about that. *We could have everybody vote. From the feeds. Instantaneous. Then it would be a democracy.*

Except, she said, *only about seventy-three percent of Americans have feeds.*

Oh, I said. *Yeah.* And so I felt stupid. *There's that many who don't?*

Then she told me, *I didn't used to have a feed.*

I was like, *What do you mean?*

She was quiet like she didn't want to chat. It was that kind of quiet. Then she went, *We didn't have enough money. When I was little. And my dad and mom didn't want me to have one.*

Holy shit.

I got it when I was seven.

I'm sorry, I said.

For what?

For not knowing. You know, that so many people don't have them.

No one with feeds thinks about it, she said. *When you have the feed all your life, you're brought up to not think about things. Like them never telling you that it's a republic and not a democracy. It's something that makes me angry, what people don't know about these days. Because of the feed, we're raising a nation of idiots. Ignorant, self-centered idiots.*

Suddenly, she realized what she had said, that she'd just called me a self-centered, ignorant idiot. She stopped. She started stumbling all over her words, and she was like, *I didn't mean . . . I, you know . . . it's not really important, but just, I believe . . . ,* and so on. I just sat there and watched her. I could tell I was liking to watch her trip up over her words while I was doing this angry face, so I didn't move my mouth or chat her or anything. I just sat, and she felt bad, and then she even chatted me, *I'm sorry,* which was bad, because it showed that we both knew I was stupid, and then I looked away. I looked away, and she put her hand on my arm, which was the worst, because it was the consolation prize.

That night, when I got home, I was looking out the window, being sorry, and my mother was like, "What's wrong?"

I didn't answer for a while. Finally, I said, "Do you think I'm stupid? I mean, am I dumb?"

"You're a nontraditional learner."

Smell Factor said, "No, he's not. He's dumb."

My mother asked, "Is this re: Violet?"

"No."

"Come on. Is it re: her? Because she shouldn't make you feel stupid. That's not good."

"Mom, it's un-re: her, okay?"

"She should be proud of you."

I didn't want to say anything. I didn't want my mom to think Violet was a snob. Violet wasn't a snob. I was just dumb.

My mom came over and said to me, "You're a wonderful boy. I know I'm your mom, but I can say that you're a wonderful boy. Isn't he, Steve?"

My dad was conked out at the table going over the news on the feed, but he pulled himself up, and she was like, "Isn't he a wonderful boy?," and my dad was like, "Sure, yeah, yeah," and my mom was like, "You're as handsome as a duck in butter."

"Where does she live, anyway?" my dad asked.

"I don't know. Like, two hundred miles from here. I've never been there. Why?"

"Just asking."

"You're a catch," said my mother. "You're pewter."

That was no help at all, and the next day, I did really bad on a test, and I came home, and Violet chatted me to say she couldn't talk, she was, I don't know, learning ancient Swahili or building a replica of Carthage out of iron filings or finding the cure for entropy or some shit, and I was sitting around, staring at a corner of a room, where two of the walls and the floor came together, and my mom and dad caught me doing it, and my mom came up and hugged me.

I could tell it was all staged. They'd tried to find me. I patted Mom a little on the back, enough to say, *Okay, yeah, enough for affection. You can back off now, Ma.* She did, and I hoped they would leave, but they weren't done. So I had to sit there and listen to about me.

She said, "You're just the boy we wanted. You're good enough for any girl. You're just what we asked for."

My dad was meg uncomfortable and kept on moving from foot to foot.

My mom ran her fingers through my hair, and

rocked me back and forth, even though I was standing, and she said, like a poem, "You've got your father's eyes and my nose."

"And my mouth," said my dad.

"And my hands," said my mom.

"And the chin, dimples, and hairline of DelGlacey Murdoch."

"What?" I said.

"This big actor," explained my mom. "We thought he was like the most beautiful man we'd ever seen in our lives."

"Well," said my dad, "we *thought* he was going to be big."

"We saw a feedcast with him in it the night we . . . the night you were made." My mom winked.

"What?" I said. "What was his name? You never told me about the actor."

"He was . . . What did you say his name was again, Steve?"

"DelGlacey Murdoch."

"DelGlacey Murdoch," said my mom, kind of smoothing things over. "That's right. And we thought he was the most beautiful man we'd ever seen. So after the movie we went right to the conceptionarium and told them, 'We want the most beautiful boy you've ever made. We want him with my nose and his dad's eyes, and for the rest, we have this picture of DelGlacey Murdoch.'"

I said, "I've never even like *heard* of DelGlacey Murdoch."

My father played nervously with his pin-stripes. "He didn't . . . he didn't really take off the way like we expected. After that movie, he was mostly . . . I guess . . . small roles."

"He starred in some things," said my mom. "Steve, he starred in a lot of things."

"Straight to daytime," said my dad.

"Honey, he was the most beautiful actor ever. So we went into the conceptionarium, and told the geneticists what we wanted, and your father went in one room, and I went in the other, and . . ."

"Hey—hey—I don't want to hear!"

"You know what he was in?" said my dad. "Remember *Virtual Blast*? He played the fifth Navy Seal, with the croup. You know, coughing."

"He was in the feature with all the crazy utensils," said my mother. "A few years ago? That one? He was the doorman in the pillbox hat."

I had already pulled up a list of his feed-features and I was going over them. None of them got more than two stars. My parents were checking my feed, I could feel them like prodding it, and my mom was like, "It doesn't matter what he was in," and she m-chatted something to my dad, and so he was like, "No, no, that isn't the point."

"What we're talking about," said my mother,

"is how handsome you are, and how brave you are."

"We've decided that you've been through a lot," said my father.

"You've been very brave," my mother repeated.

"Yeah . . . ?" I said. "I just fell down. The guy touched me and I just like, fell down."

"You were brave," said my father.

"We've decided you need a little cheering up," said my mother.

I started to feel a little better. I could feel their feeds shifting toward a common point, some kind of banner they were pulling up.

"We've decided to get you your own upcar," said my mother.

"You can pick it," said my dad. "Within certain limits."

"Oh, god!" I said. "Oh, god! Oh, Mom— Dad—this is—oh, shit! Holy shit! Are you kidding! You are like the best mom and dad ever!"

"We're not kidding," said my dad. "Here's the banner."

And it unwrapped in my head, a banner for a dealer, and links to other dealers, and a big line of credit, and I was hugging them, and I was like holy shit, by tomorrow I would be driving to pick up Violet in my own goddamn upcar, and suddenly, suddenly, I didn't feel so stupid anymore.

○ ○ ○

"... what the President meant in the intercepted
chat. This was, uh, nothing but a routine
translation problem. It has to be understood,
that . . . It has to be understood that when the
President referred to the Prime Minister of the
Global Alliance as a 'big shithead,' what he
was trying to convey was, uh—this is an
American idiom used to praise people, by
referring to the sheer fertilizing power of their
thoughts. The President meant to say that the
Prime Minister's head was fertile, just full of
these nutrients where ideas can grow. It really
was a compliment. We should say again that
any attempt to withdraw the Alliance's
diplomatic presence from American soil will
be taken as a sign of ill will, and, uh, we are
likely to respond with the most stringent . . ."

○ ○ ○

lift

My father took me to test-drive upcars on Saturday. I had tried a lot of them in the feed-sim, but it's not the same as actually driving them, and you should always test-drive a vehicle before purchasing it, because you never know what unexpected factors will come into play. For example, I discovered that the Illia Cloud had a windshield that was kind of the wrong height for me, and I didn't like the dashboard arrangement of the Dodge Cormorant.

We picked Violet up at the mall and took her with us. Both she and me were really excited by the whole thing, and we were chatting really fast the whole time, about what color to get, and whether the red was too cheesy, or whether it was autumnal, which is what she said.

We took them out to test-drive, with my

father sitting next to me. He'd be chatting with someone somewhere else while I drove. He'd be looking out the window, and wincing whenever Violet or I talked out loud. He had trouble thinking and hearing at the same time. When he was done chatting, he'd ask me a question out loud, like, "How's she feel?"

Violet would tell me, "Resist the feed. Look into ox carts."

"Yeah, thanks, Violet," my father would say. "We're having serious decision flux here." He'd ask me, "What do you think?"

I'd tell him about the handling or the lift.

Violet would say, "How about a howdah?"

Dad asked, "What's a howdah?"

"A seat on elephant-back."

"Great. Great. Thanks."

Me and Violet walked up and down the rows of upcars. I was thinking about the Swarp and the Dodge Gryphon.

The Swarp didn't have as much room in the back. It was a little sportier.

The Dodge Gryphon had the larger back seat for your friends and shit, but it was a little lumbering.

So here was the decision: Dodge was bannering me with me driving, and all of these people in bikinis stuffed into the car with me, this big party, and with a beach ball, too, like I could be the scene; and Nongen, who made the Swarp, was showing a romantic drive through the mountains with just me and Violet, who they got pretty much right, except they made her taller and with bigger boobs, and they made her cheeks kind of sparkly in a way that, if it were really happening, I would try to wipe off with a facecloth.

I didn't know which to choose, because if I got an upcar that was too small, then Link and Marty might be like, "We'll take my car instead. More of us can fit in," and then I would have spent these hundreds of thousands of dollars for nothing. But if I bought the Swarp, it was a little more sporty, and that might be brag, because the Dodge Gryphon was maybe too family.

"So you're getting this as a reward for being in the hospital?" Violet asked.

"I guess."

"A little present from Mommy and Daddy?"

"Yeah. They're buying it."

She thought about this for a minute. Then she shook her head. "You're lucky."

"Are you saying I'm spoiled?"

"No."

"It seems like that's what you mean."

"No, that's not it."

I thought for a second, and said, "So what is it?"

"Nothing."

"Look, it's like a reward. I'm going to turn in evidence in court and everything. I mean, you are, too, but we're going to have to go to court against that guy. We should get something for that. We deserve it."

She looked at me strangely.

"What?" I said.

"No one's told you?"

I waited. Her eyebrow was arched. Finally, I gave in and said, "No. No one told me what?"

"We're not going to court."

"We got out of it? My dad was trying to get us out of it."

"He didn't need to. The guy was dead."

"What? How?"

"He died a day after we went into the hospital. Contusions. Broken skull."

"What are contusions?" I looked it up. "Oh."

"He was beaten to death at the club. We saw it. The police, remember? They beat him over the head."

She reached out and took my arm.

My father walked toward us across the pavement, waving. The plastic flags were flapping in the artificial wind while Muzak came out of heaven.

I bought the Dodge.

a question of moral

That night we all had dinner together, my family and Violet. My dad was real proud of me, and was all, "He drove home behind me. Can you like believe this shit? Our own son with his own upcar?"

I couldn't stop smiling. "Yeah." I was like, "It's meg brag." My mom smiled at me.

Smell Factor wasn't listening to anything. He had some crappy kids' music show blasting in his feed so loud his aud nerves were probably shot. He had a bunny plate and was making something with his burrito.

"Are you going to take Violet out in it?" Mom asked.

"Tomorrow. She and me are driving out to like the country. She wants to go for a walk. I'm picking her up." I couldn't help grinning like a shithead again.

Violet smiled back at me.

"There's a forest," said Violet. "It's called Jefferson Park. We're thinking about going either there, or out to beef country."

My dad nodded. "It'll have to be beef country," he said. "The forest's gone."

"Jefferson Park?"

He nodded, then squinted while he like clawed something off the roof of his mouth with his tongue. He told us, "Yeah. Jefferson Park? Yeah. That was knocked down to make an air factory."

"You're kidding!" said Violet.

"Yeah, that's what happened," said Dad, shrugging. "You got to have air."

Violet pointed out, "Trees make air," which kind of worried me because I knew Dad would think it was snotty.

My father stared at her for a long time. Then he said, "Yeah. Sure. Do you know how inefficient trees are, next to an air factory?"

"But we need trees!"

"For what?" he said. "I mean, they're nice, and it's too bad, but like . . . Do you know how much real estate costs?"

"I can't believe they cut it down!"

Mom said to Smell Factor, "Hey. Hey! Stop playing with your food."

Smell Factor was head-banging with the feed music and turning his bunny plate around and around with his little pudgy fingers.

My father told him, "This is dinner together. That means family networking and defragging time."

"They cut down Jefferson Park? That is so like corporate—"

My father nodded and smiled at her with this meg condescending smile on his face, and was like, "Dude, I remember when I was like you. You should grow up to be a, you know. Clean-air worker or something. Don't lose that. But remember. It's about people. People need a lot of air."

For a minute, we all ate without saying anything. Violet looked either angry or embarrassed. I chatted her about being sorry for what Dad said, but she didn't chat me back. I thought Dad was being kind of a jerk to Violet. I wanted to say something, like, something that would be, you know, something about how she was more right than he was. I said, "Hey, Violet told me we're not going to court."

"About what?" my mother said.

"We were like assaulted?" I said. "Remember? The thing on the moon?"

"Yeah, sure," said my dad. "No, he's dead. There's no trial. We've all talked about suing.

We'll probably sue the nightclub, maybe the police."

I said, "No one told me he was dead."

My father chewed some.

Smell Factor was banging his head and singing along with the feed, "Intercrural or oral. Ain't a question of moral."

My father said to me, "There wasn't any reason for you to know."

"Yes, there was."

"No, there wasn't."

"It's my feed."

"You'd just get worried."

"I want to get worried. If there's like some meg thing wrong."

"Intercrural or oral! Ain't a question of moral!"

My mom reached over and touched me on the wrist and said, "You're safe."

Dad said, "You have an upcar."

"The lunatic is dead," said my mother. "There's nothing to worry about."

Violet said, "It was frightening for all of us."

"Yeah, sure," said Dad, dismissing her kind of jerkily, "but that's no reason—"

"Intercrural or oral! Ain't a question of moral!"

"Smell Factor!"

"That's not his name," said my mother.

"Intercrural or oral! Ain't a question of moral!"

"What would you—"

"Intercrural or oral! Ain't a question of moral!"

"Hey!" yelled my mother. "Hey, you! We don't sing at the table!"

"You're acting out of line," said my father, pointing at me. "I'm really disappointed."

"Doing what?" I said. "I'm just asking."

"Dude, I just bought you an upcar, and you're being a brat."

You're not being a brat, Violet chatted.

"Stop chatting," said my dad. "What are you saying?"

"Let them alone, Steve," said Mom.

Suddenly, I saw Violet freeze, and her eyes stopped moving and her face got all white.

My dad was saying, "Look, we're going to sue the nightclub. Okay?"

"Sure," I said. "Whatev."

"Quits?"

"Quits."

"Now maybe you better take the girlf home. In the new upcar. With the keys I just held out in my palm like a gift. Oh, because it was a gift."

My father got up all pissy and took the dishes into the kitchen. He rattled them against the rim of the junktube as he threw them away. They crashed down into the thing, the incinerator.

"You okay?" I said to Violet. "We should go."

"It's just, my foot's fallen asleep."

"Shake it," I said.

She looked down at the table. *I mean my foot isn't working. Don't say anything. It's happened a couple of times since the hack. Something just won't work for an hour or two. My finger or something.*

I was like, *Holy shit. Are you okay?*

I'm fine.

Do you want some water?

Titus, don't worry about it. It'll go away in a minute. It was just the stress.

Try to move the foot. Just try.

She just sat there, smiling kind of sick, not moving while right next to her Mom and Smell Factor crinkled up the disposable table together and threw it away. Violet was still in her chair, near where the table had been. She was alone in the middle of the rug.

Finally, she moved the foot. She moved it slowly in circles. She breathed out really deep. Her eyes were closed, like it was sex.

I held out my hand and pulled her to her feet. She came to my arms like we were doing some kind of flamenco rumpus. My mom smiled, and my dad, who was still pissed, said, "Yeah. Cute."

We left a few minutes later. I drove her most of the way to her house, and we met her father in a mall parking lot. It was a new mall, with lots of

129

spotlights swinging through the sky and rainbows going up a giant pyramid. We had to wait a few minutes for her dad to get there. We just sat together, holding hands. In my new Dodge Gryphon.

I asked, "Are you sure you're okay?"

"I'm fine. It goes away."

I leaned my head against the window. We were quiet.

She was looking at her knees. She asked me, "What are you thinking about?"

I looked behind us. I sighed, and I was drumming my fingers on the steering column and all. I said, "What if it really doesn't handle as good? You know, it's roomier, but what if it doesn't handle as good as the Swarp?"

She nodded. She said, "Are you at least okay with the color?"

"It's a good red," I said. "I guess."

"Autumnal," she said. "It's nice."

"You're sure it's not like cheap?"

"It's fall-like."

I smiled. "Thanks."

She said, "I'm a peach."

"Yeah. You're a peach."

Her father was landing. I couldn't see him through the glare of his windshield. She got out of the car. She kissed me. I said I would see her the next morning.

She kept turning and waving as she walked away across the pavement. The spotlights wobbled over the Clouds™. The pyramid glowed. I rose up into the sky and turned the feed on to songs about people allowed to get out of the same bed, and to eat breakfast together, two toasts on the very same plate.

o o o

'Cause if love
    Can't help us from above,
    Can't help us like a dove,
    With wings so full of love,
    Then let me go.

And if hope
    Is nothing but a dope
    Who's holding on to rope
    Then I don't think I can cope,
    So let me go,
    Darling,
    Let me go.

But . . .
    But, if faith
    Is more than just a wraith
    And is in real good faith
    Then let us both have faith
    And hold me tight.

'Cause "touching"
    Is not just that it's touching,
    But that we both are touching,
    Like with our mouths are touching,
    So hold me tight,

Darling,
    Hold me tight.

Ho-oh-old me tight.

Hold me tight.

Hold me tight.

o   o   o

observe the
remarkable
verdure

The next day, I followed my feed's directions to her house. I drove about two hundred miles to get to the general area. It was a good day for a walk in the country, because there were these big occasional Clouds™, but mostly blue. The sun was reflecting in darts off all the upcars that passed me.

Her neighborhood was down a long droptube. I kept on going down and down through all these different suburbs, called Fox Glen and Caleby Farm Estates and Waterview Park, until I hit the bottom of the tube, where it was called Creville Heights.

Creville Heights was all one big area, instead of each yard having its own bubble with its own sun and seasons. They must've had just one sun for the whole place. All the houses were really old and flat. The streets were blue and cracked, and they were streets, I mean, like for when things went on the ground. Their sun was up and you could see the sky was peeling.

I found her house, which was a little house with her parents' upcar parked outside it and some kind of a sculpture in the yard, with some hoops or loops and a floating, spiky ball.

I parked next to the house with the upcar still levitated, and I climbed down and went to the door. The doorbell played a piece of music, which I could hear through the door, which was wood.

She came to the door, and she was all smiling, and she was so glad to see me, and I was glad to see her. She invited me in to meet her dad, who was at home. I went in.

The place was a mess. Everything had words on it. There were papers with words on them, and books, and even posters on the wall had words. Her father looked like a crank. He was sitting in a lawn chair in the living room, hunched over like a hunchback, sorting puzzle pieces. His back honestly had a big hunch, which was from a really, really early feedscanner, from back when they wore them in a big backpack on their back, with special glasses that had foldout screens on either side of your eyes. He wore the glasses, too, and when we shook hands I could see pictures and words reflecting on his eyeballs, like when you stir water in the sun.

He held out his hand. He said, "It is a fine

pleasure to meet you and make your acquaintance." He had a very slight smile, which didn't change when he moved his mouth. He spoke with this buzzing, flat kind of voice. He said, "I am filled with astonishment at the regularity of your features and the handsome generosity you have shown my daughter. The two of you are close, which gladdens the heart, as close as twin wings torn off the same butterfly."

Violet said, "You can see why I don't take him out in public much."

"The sarcasm of my daughter notwithstanding, it is nonetheless an occasion of great moment to meet one of her erotic attachments. In the line of things, she has not brought them home, but has chosen instead to conduct her trysts at remote locales, perhaps beach huts or oxygen-rich confabularies."

"The surprising thing is," said Violet, "when he flunked out of charm school, it was because he couldn't learn the minuet."

"She meets them at the drama, I presume, or speakeasies."

"Why don't we leave," Violet suggested, "while my last shred of dignity is still at least as big as a thong?"

I was like, "It was . . . It was real good to meet you." I said, "We're going out into the country for the day. I'll take real good care of her." I was trying to be like a man to another man, like responsible.

He nodded. He flattened his hand, and lifted off with it like it was a Dodge Gryphon, and he was making an engine noise, and then he flew his hand toward some books and landed it. He made these chirpy noises like the windows rolling down. He said in a high-pitched voice, like a teensy-weensy kind of voice, "Ooooooh! Observe the remarkable verdure! Little friend, I am master of all I survey."

I nodded. Violet had the door opened. We went out and climbed into the Gryphon. We pulled on our seat belts.

"Wow," I said.

"Yeah."

I lifted us off and we floated down the street.

"He's something."

"So far as my social life goes, what strikes me as a good idea is leaving him in the basement wrapped in a cocoon of pink insulation."

"I didn't understand a single thing he said."

"He says the language is dying. He thinks words are being debased. So he tries to speak entirely in weird words and irony, so no one can simplify anything he says."

We turned a corner.

"Where's your mom?" I asked.

"Probably South America," Violet said. "She likes it warm."

"Are they divorced?"

"They never married."

"Your life . . . It must be kind of strange?"

"Meaning what?"

"Just . . . it's not . . . the things that most of us . . . do?"

"No," she said, like she wanted to change the topic.

I hit the droptube, and we fell up.

a day
in the country

We flew for an hour or so out into farm country.

While we flew, she told me the story of her family, which was that her mom and dad met when they were in grad school, and decided to live together as an experiment in lifestyle, and had her. Then everything was fine for a few years, but when she was about six or seven her parents started like fighting all the time, and yelling all the time and stuff, and her mother ran away. I asked her if that was when her father started to get like he was, I mean, hard to understand, and she said he was always hard to understand, but after her mother left was when he started to get completely like he was.

She played me some saved memories of him lecturing. He was pacing up and down through the lecture hall and he was saying, "In the nineties, the older programming languages, with their emphasis on neoclassical, even Aristotelian logical structures, gave way to object-oriented interactive structures." His shoes scraped along the tiled floor. He looked all his students in the eye, like he was challenging them to a fight. He leaned toward them and said, "In object-oriented programming, discrete software objects interfaced more freely, in a system of corporate service provision that mirrored the emergent structures of late capitalism." Who the hell knows what he meant, but suddenly, he seemed kind of powerful, like someone who shouldn't necessarily be wound up in a cocoon of pink insulation and hidden in a basement somewhere. He was like a different guy.

She said the only time he actually talked like a normal human being was sometimes when he was big tired and they were eating dinner before he went to bed.

She and he took turns making dinner.

They had just got a Kitchnet food synthesizer.

She asked for my family's story, but it wasn't as interesting. Just *da da da,* my parents met through some friend, *da da da,* they went out, they started to live together, *da da da,* they went to Venus, *da da da,* you know, they're sitting in this restaurant on Venus, back when Venus was called *The Love Planet,* with *Love* pronounced *Lerv,* back before the moulting-quakes and the uprisings, so they're sitting there, and my dad holds up his hand, and it has this big lump on one of the fingers, like some kind of cyst? And my mom's like, *Steve, what's that, is it malignant?* and he goes, *Honey, I hope it's benign,* and he pulls a little pull-tab and the skin unpeels and under it is an engagement ring for her, already on his finger! So he takes it off and slips it on her finger and it constricts and clamps on and she's like, *Omigod! Omigod!* and everyone in the restaurant starts clapping. And she's like, *No, I don't have any like circulation to my finger,* and so they had to go to a jeweler really quick and get it adjusted, which is why whenever they have a fight and make up, my mom always has this joke? She goes, *Yup, married, and with the scars to prove it.*

It felt good to hear Violet's story, and to tell mine, even though hers was kind of more interesting than mine. I said it must be hard for her dad to bring her up and home-school her himself. She said it was, that he worked real hard at it, and also worked real hard teaching. She was proud of him, even though he was—from what I could see? like, in my opinion?—an insane psychopath.

Our feeds caught a banner from a farm that invited visitors, where you could walk around and see everything grow, so we swerved for there and landed. There weren't many other people there that day, so we were almost alone while we walked around.

It was real peaceful. We walked along holding hands, and our elbows rubbed, too. Violet wasn't wearing sleeves, so I could see the little frowns made by her elbows.

It smelled like the country. It was a filet mignon farm, all of it, and the tissue spread for miles around the paths where we were walking. It was like these huge hedges of red all around us, with these beautiful marble patterns running through them. They had these tubes, they were bringing the tissue blood, and we could see the blood running around, up and down. It was really interesting. I like to see how things are made, and to understand where they come from.

It was a perfect afternoon. They had made part of it into a steak maze, for tourists, and we split up in the steak maze and tried to see who could get to the center first. We were like running around corners and peeking and diving, and there were these mirrors set up to confuse you, so you'd see all these nonexistent beef hallways. We were big laughing and we'd run into each other and growl and back away. There were other tourists in the steak maze, too, and they thought we were cute.

Then we sat and had some cider doughnuts that we bought at the farm stand. We got some that were plain and some cinnamon. I liked the cinnamon better. Violet said that it was important to start with the plain, so that the cinnamon seemed more like a change. She said she had a theory that everything was better if you delayed it. She had this whole thing about self-control, okay, and the importance of self-control. For example, she said, when she bought something, she wouldn't let herself order it for a long time. Then she would just go to the purchase site and show it to herself. Then she'd let herself get fed the sense-sim, you know, she'd let herself know how it would feel, or what it would smell like. Then she would go away and wouldn't look for a week. Then she would go back finally and order it, but only if it was on back order and wouldn't be shipped immediately. Then finally when it was ready to ship, she'd like be, oh, hey, I don't want it shipped hour rate, I want it slow, slow rate. So it would take like three days to get to her, and then she'd leave it in the box. Finally, she'd open the box just enough to see like the hem of the skirt or whatever. She would touch it, just knowing it was hers. She'd run her fingers along it kind of delicate. Just along the edge of it, not even really letting herself touch it completely, just gently, with her fingertips, or maybe the back of her hand. She would wait for days until she couldn't stand it anymore to take it out and try it on.

At this point, I was completely turned on. I wanted to get more doughnuts, but it was this debate between getting more doughnuts, which were really good doughnuts, but not being able to stand up because I had complete prong.

So we sat for a while just where we were and I flattened out the doughnut bag with my hand on the tabletop. You could tell how good the doughnuts were because they left a clear ring on the paper.

Later, we went and climbed up an observation tower over the farm. It was getting to be sunset, so it was meg pretty.

We were sitting side by side, with our legs swinging on the wall of the tower, and the Clouds™ were all turning pink in front of us. We could see all these miles of filet mignon from where we were sitting, and some places where the genetic coding had gone wrong and there, in the middle of the beef, the tissue had formed a horn or an eye or a heart blinking up at the sunset, which was this brag red, and which hit on all those miles of muscle and made it flex and quiver, with all these shudders running across the top of it, and birds were flying over, crying kind of sad, maybe seagulls looking for garbage, and the whole thing, with the beef, and the birds, and the sky, it all glowed like there was a light inside it, which it was time to show us now.

Later, when we were flying back in the dark, lit up by the dashboard, she asked me, "If you could die any way you wanted, how would you like to?"

I said, "Why you asking?"

She said, "I've just been thinking about it a lot."

I thought for a while. Then I said, "I'd like to have this like, this intense pleasure in every one of my senses, all of them so full up that they just burst me open, and the feed like going a mile a second, so that it's like every channel is just jammed with excitement, and it's going faster and faster and better and better, until just—*BAM*! That's it, I guess. I'd like to die from some kind of sense overload."

She nodded.

I said, "I'm going to do that when I get real old and boring."

She said, "Yeah. You know, I think death is shallower now. It used to be a hole you fell into and kept falling. Now it's just a blank."

We flew over a lake. The bottom had been covered with a huge blue ad that was lit up and magnified by the water, which had a picture of a smiling brain and broadcasted "Dynacom Inc." when you looked at it.

I was like, "What are you asking for?"

She said, "It makes good times even better

when you know they're going to end. Like grilled vegetables are better because some of them are partly soot."

I wanted to point out that that was probably because her dad made them, but that if someone good makes them, they're probably not partly soot, but I didn't think that was her point, about vegetables, so I just kept flying, and I said, "This was a good time?" and she said, "One of the best," and I said, "So when it's time for them to do a pleasure overload on me, are you going to be around to give the order to cut the juice?"

She looked at me, surprised. For a second, she was like completely confused. It was like I'd said something else.

Then she saw what I meant, and she laughed like I'd given her a present. She said, "If you'll let me, sure. Sure I'll be there." She leaned over, really sudden, and kissed me on the cheek. Then she whispered, "I'll be the first one, dumpling, to pull your plug."

The way she said it, pull your plug, it sounded kind of sexy.

Right then, everything seemed perfect.

I dropped her off, and we planned other things, and did a secret handshake. I drove back toward home listening to some brag new triumph screams by British storm 'n' chunder bands. When I got home, the lights were out, but they came on for me. I walked through the empty house, and got ready for bed, and lay there thinking about how perfect everything was.

I could feel my family all around me. I could trace their feeds faintly, because they weren't shielding them. Smell Factor was dreaming while a fun-site with talking giraffes sang him songs and showed him wonderful things in different shapes. My parents were upstairs going in mal, which they wouldn't want me to know, but which I could tell, because they chose a really flashy, expensive malfunction site that was easy to trace. They were winding down together, I guess. Like, you can only go on being completely fugue-stressed for so long without winding down.

I could feel all of my family asleep in their own way around me, in the empty house, in our bubble, where we could turn on and off the sun and the stars, and the feed spoke to me real quiet about new trends, about pants that should be shorter or longer, and bands I should know, and games with new levels and stalactites and fields of diamonds, and friends of many colors were all drinking Coke, and beer was washing through mountain passes, and the stars of the *Oh? Wow! Thing!* had got lesions, so lesions were hip now, real hip, and mine looked like a million dollars. The sun was rising over foreign countries, and underwear was cheap, and there were new techniques to reconfigure pecs, abs, and nipples, and the President of the United States was certain of the future, and at Weatherbee & Crotch there was a sale banner and nice rugby shirts and there were pictures of freckled prep-school boys and girls in chinos playing on the beach and dry humping in the eel grass, and as I fell asleep, the feed murmured to me again and again: *All shall be well . . . and all shall be well . . . and all manner of things shall be well.*

o o o

. . . First, in the deserts and veldts arose oral
    culture, the culture of the spoken word. Then
    in the cities with their temples and bazaars
    came the pictographs, and later, symbols that
    produced sounds as if by magic, and what
    followed was written culture. Then, in the
    universities and under the steeples of young
    nations, print culture. These—oral culture,
    written culture, the culture of print—these
    have always been considered the great epochs
    of man.

But we have entered a new age. We are a new
    people. It is now the age of oneiric culture, the
    culture of dreams.

And we are the nation of dreams. We are seers. We
    are wizards. We speak in visions. Our letters
    are like flocks of doves, released from under
    our hats. We have only to stretch out our hand
    and desire, and what we wish for settles like a
    kerchief in our palm. We are a race of
    sorcerers, enchanters. We are Atlantis. We are
    the wizard-isle of Mu.

What we wish for, is ours.

It is the age of oneiric culture. And we, America,
we are the nation of dreams.

o   o   o

nudging
again

Later that night, I had nightmares.

Someone was poking my head with a broom handle. They tried to put it like in my ear. They said, "Whispering makes a narrow place narrower."

Then came all these pictures, and I was seeing all over the world, and there were explanations, but I was still asleep, and I couldn't figure them out. I saw khakis that were really cheap, only $150, but I didn't like the stitching, and then I saw them torn and there was blood on them. It was a riot on a street, and people were screaming in some other language, they were in khakis or jeans and T-shirts, and hey were throwing stones and bottles, and the police were moving forward on horses, and a man in the crowd waved a gun, and then the firing started. They were in front of factories, and clouds of gas drifted through them and the American flags they were burning started to spark big, and the gas got darker and darker, and the people sped up, like a joke, grabbing at their necks and waving and sitting and slapping the ground. They fell down. I saw a sign with a picture of a head with a little devil sitting in the brain, inside the skull, with these like energy bolts coming out of his mouth.

I saw fields and fields of black, it was this disgusting black shit, spread for miles. I saw walls of concrete fall from the sky and crush little wood houses. I saw a furry animal trying to stand up on its legs but the back ones were broken or not working, and it dragged itself with the front ones, whimpering, through someplace with gray dust, and needles coming out of the sand. Its jaws were open. I saw long cables going through the sea. I saw girls sewing things, little girls in big halls. I saw people praying over missiles. I smelled the summer in this rocky place, and the summer smelled like electrical burns. I saw a kid looking at me, he was a kid from another culture, where they wear dresses, and there were all of these shadows all over his face, these amazing shadows, and I thought it was a really cool picture, to get all of those weird shadows somehow, but with nothing making them, and finally, I realized that they weren't shadows, they were bruises, and then the end of a gun, it's called the butt, it came down and hit him in the face and then all the pictures were over.

Hey, Violet said. *Hey. Was that you?*

I was like, *What? What's the thing? With . . . the . . . ?*

Did I wake you up?

Okay, could . . . is she . . . ?

Hey—look lively. Someone was just nosing around my feed, checking out my specs and sending me all these images.

It was probably a corp. Don't . . . Oh, unit, I can't believe you completely jolted me. I was having this weird-ass dreaming.

I don't think it was a corp. They didn't have a tag.

Don't you have a shield?

They got right wham through the shield.

Oh, unit. Oh, unit. I'm . . . Do you know how asleep I was?

I called FeedTech Customer Assistance. I'm going to report this. Something's happening.

Oh, okay. Shit. Okay. So can I go like back to sleep?

You sure it wasn't you?

Unette—it wasn't me. I was so asleep, it was like . . . It was like ten asleep factor.

They can trace who it was, I bet.

Yeah. Maybe.

You didn't see any of this? The images?

What of?

There's someone else here. Can you feel it?

Who?

Someone else. They just tapped in, just a second ago.

A voice said, *Hi, this is Nina from FeedTech Customer Assistance.*

Thank god.

Are you tired of the same old shoulders? Why not try extensions?

Violet was like, *Someone just approached my feed. They were checking the specs and stats.*

And what can I do to help you this morning?

You need to follow them and see, somehow, see who it was. Quickly . . . Quickly!

Violet, I'd love to respond personally to each and every request for assistance, but unfortunately I'm unable to, due to increased customer demand, so I've sent this automated intelligence Nina to talk to you instead.

No, you don't understand.

Looking at your recent purchase history, I notice that you've expressed interest in a lot of products you haven't bought. Are you having trouble making up your mind with so much cool stuff to choose from?

Can you please connect me with a live operator?

Violet, I think I can help you come up with

products that really say, "You." They'll shout, "You! You! You!" as if it was always Saturday! Oh, I know! You're almost a woman, and you want things that are totally big Violet! That's where I can help!

All right, chatted Violet. *No thanks. Thanks. I'm done.*

Sometimes choices are hard to make.

Fuck off.

This automated intelligence Nina can help you throw away the bad—and find the good! I can help you find the great products that are uniquely the woman known as "Ms. Violet Durn"!

Fuck off!

Okay, it doesn't seem like you want to talk right now. So I'm going back to my little hole. There, I'll be sorting and sifting, and trying to make life as easy and interesting as possible for you and your friend and all of our excellent customers at FeedTech— making your dreams into hard fact™.

Okay. Thanks. Thanks a big lot.

And thank you, Violet Durn of 1421 Applebaum Avenue. I'll look forward to helping you again, whenever you—

Can I go back to sleep? I asked. *I had these really weird dreams.*

Violet seemed kind of without any energy. She was like, *Go ahead. I'll talk to you tomorrow.*

We said good night. She was slow. I turned over and curled up, and the pictures playing in my head now were better, not so violent or sucky. They were more of women in turtlenecks petting my hair. I heard some music. I fell asleep. It was a deep sleep, and I didn't wake up until morning.

It is an upcar tearing along over the desert. It cuts
    brag swerves through passes and over
    gulches.

*Someone once said it was easier for a camel to pass
    through the eye of a needle than for a rich guy
    to get into heaven.*

There is a city. A marketplace. Camels. Arabs.
    The upcar shoots overhead, and they duck.

*Yeah, sure. Now we know that the "eye of the
    needle" is just another name for a gate in
    Jerusalem—and with the Swarp XE-11's
    mega-lepton lift and electrokinetic gyrostasis,
    you can flip ninety degrees to the ground and
    back again in one-point-two seconds—so
    getting through the gate just won't be a
    problem anymore.*

The Swarp XE-11: You can take it with you.

the real thing

One Saturday, a few days after we saw the riot from the news in our dreams, there was this promotion, where if you talked about the great taste of Coca-Cola to your friends like a thousand times, you got a free six-pack of it, so we decided to take them for some meg ride by all getting together and being like, *Coke, Coke, Coke, Coke* for about three hours so we'd get a year's supply. It was a chance to rip off the corporations, which we all thought was a funny idea.

I picked up Violet at her house and we drove to Marty's, where everyone was meeting.

When we got there, Calista and Loga were getting out of Calista's car, and it was like, *Whoa*, because they were wearing all torn-up clothes. They were walking normal, but they looked like they'd been burned up and hit with stuff.

I ran over to them. I was going, "Holy shit!

Are you okay? What happened?" and Violet, too, she was going, "Hey—are you okay?"

They stood there and looked at us, then looked at each other like, *Omigod! Someone is poopiehead!*

"Yuh," said Loga. "It's Riot Gear. It's retro. It's beat up to look like one of the big twentieth-century riots. It's been big since earlier this week."

I was like, "Oh."

Violet was like, "Sorry."

"No wrong," said Calista, flipping her hair.

When we went inside, Marty and Quendy were also wearing Riot Gear. Everyone was going, *Hi! Hey! Hey! Hi! Unit! What's doing?*

"Hey!" said Loga to Quendy, pointing. "Kent State collection, right? Great skirt!"

Quendy bowed her legs out. "It's not a skirt—it's culottes!"

"Ohhh, cute!"

Calista said, "That looks great on you!"

Quendy didn't say anything to Calista, because Calista had just put her arm around Link and they were smelling each other's faces, and Quendy was jealous.

"Units!" said Marty. "Into the—in here—fuck yeah, man—into the living room. Kay kay kay kay. Right in here."

We grabbed some seats.

"Okay," said Marty. "O-fuckin'-kay!" He nodded. "Coca-Cola!"

We waited to start.

We were like waiting.

We all sat there for a minute, looking like we were smiling, but in reality, not. Each of us looked at everyone else's face. Violet chatted me, *This is like when I was twelve, and we had this slumber party and agreed to show each other our boobs. I think we finally just gave up and watched* America's Unlikeliest Allergy Attacks.

"So . . . ," said Marty, kind of sneaky. "Anyone up for the great taste of . . . Coke?"

Loga said, "I like its refreshing flavor."

"It's really good on a really hot day," said Link. "There's nothing like an ice-cold Coke."

"I like regular Coke," said Quendy, "but also the fantastic taste of Diet Coke."

Link pinched Calista. She kind of sighed, "Me, too."

Marty said, "Coke, its great taste, it's so good that I would beat up a guy if he had one and I really wanted it."

"Anyone?" said Link. "You and Coke?"

Loga said, "Coke, it's really good, almost as good as Pepsi."

"Unette!" said Marty. "'Almost'? You just lost us one! The fuckin' count just went down."

I said quickly, "I like Coke because of the energy."

Link pinched Calista. She kind of sighed, "Me, too."

Violet said, "I love the great feeling of Coke's carbonation going down my throat, all the pain, like . . ." She waved her hands in the air and looked at the ceiling, trying to think of something. She said, "It's like sweet gravel. It's like a bunch of itsy-bitsy commuters running for a shuttle in my windpipe." Everyone was looking at her. I could feel them chatting each other, saying that was stupid. I sat nearer to her. I put my hand on her back.

She was saying, "Sometimes I try to think back to the first time I ever had Coke. Because it must have hurt, but I can't remember. How could we ever have started to enjoy it? If something's an acquired taste, like, how do you start to acquire it? For that matter, who gave me Coke the first time? My father? I don't think so. Who would hand a kid a Coke and think, 'Her first one. I'm so proud.' How do we even start?"

There was a long, silent part.

Then Marty said, "Yeah. That may have cost us a few. Hey, how about the great foaming capabilities of Coke?"

And then we were onto this whole thing,

about Coke fights, and Coke floats, and Coke promotions, and we went on and on and on, but Violet didn't say anything else, just sat there silently. The guys kept going. I was laughing extra loud at everything, because I didn't want people to notice that Violet was all clammy. So I was yelling all these carbonation things and trying to bring her back in, and the other guys were going spastic and throwing pillows at each other. We were like rum and Coke, stadium Coke, flat Coke, bottled Coke, Coke and nachos, Coke and hot dogs, hot Coke, Cherry Coke, Coke on tap, comparative suckiness of, until finally there was another quiet part, and Link said, "Hey, Marty-unit, do you actually have any Coke?"

Marty was like, "No. But, fuck, aren't you getting like meg thirsty? With all of this talking about the great taste of Coke?"

We looked at our feet for a minute. I moved my butt around on the, it's called an ottoman.

"Let's go out and get some," said Link.

"Yeah. Let's go to the store."

"Which store?"

"There's a Halt 'n' Buy up on like, near the Sports Giant."

We were all standing up. Marty was like announcing, "Okay, we'll go out and get some of the great beverage of Coke, with its refreshing flavor," but no one was really rattling that way now.

Loga and Calista were whispering to each other, with Violet walking behind them. They saw she was near them, and they changed the subject.

"Oh, and omigod!" said Calista. "Are those the Stonewall Clogs? They're so brag."

"Yeah," said Loga.

"Omigod. They look wholly comfy. Are they comfy?"

"They're pretty comfy." Loga picked up her foot and played with her flowery clog, and she was like, "I got a size seven, but it feels more like a man's size seven."

"This top is the Watts Riot top."

Violet said, "I can never keep any of the riots straight. Which one was the Watts riot?"

Calista and Loga stopped and looked at her. I could feel them flashing chat.

"Like, a riot," said Calista. "I don't know, Violet. Like, when people start breaking windows and beating each other up, and they have to call in the cops. A riot. You know. Riot?"

"Oh, I just thought you might . . . know. . . . Maybe . . . I wondered what incited it." Violet was playing quickly with her own hands.

"Yeah," said Calista.

"I was just asking," said Violet.

"Okay."

"I was just . . ."

"Yeah. 'Incited.'"

"What? It's not like I was saying something mean or stupid."

"No. Okay. Loga, are we going?"

They kept on walking.

Loga said, "Put *that* in your metizabism."

Calista said, "What's a metizabism?"

"Oh, sorry. I thought it was good to use stupid, long words that no one can understand."

Calista laughed and looked backward, going, "Shhh. She'll hear you and have an alpoduffin . . . fleatcher."

In my head, I was like, *Oh shit.*

Violet was chatting me. *Did you hear that? I can't stand this anymore.*

I was like, *What do you mean?*

They were just these meg bitches. Will you take me home?

I was like, *Just let it blow. Let it blow. No wrong.*

They hate me.

No one hates you.

Your friends hate me. They think I'm stupid.

No one — fuck! — no one thinks you're stupid.

Yeah, I don't mean dumb stupid.

We can't leave them now. It would be like a total rash on their ass if we went.

They just insulted me.

Unit, they didn't.

They thought what I said during the game was stupid. They think everything I say is weird and stupid. What is your problem? Take me home.

Link was like, "You coming with?"

Violet was like, *Take me home.*

Fuck! Why? Fuck.

I want to leave.

"No," I said to Link. "Violet, uh, she has to go home."

"Unit," said Link. "The party's just begun. We haven't even filled the bathtub with anything from the kitchen yet."

"I've really got to go," said Violet, smiling like she was shaking hands with the members of the frickin' PTA.

Everyone was going out to get in their upcars and go get some stuff at the store. Calista was showing off her WTO riot Windbreaker. Violet and me said good-bye. We got in my upcar. We took off.

Then we started to fight.

fight
and
flight

I flew down the main tube in Marty's community. It was a gated community, and I waited to get out through the neighborhood's security sphincter. It pulled open, and I flew out into the droptube, going like a million miles an hour so that Violet would jerk back in her seat. Then when I was going up, I had this idea that instead of like throwing her around by going too fast, I would be like quiet angry like my father got, and I'd just do everything *exactly right,* everything up to the centigram.

So I flew really good when I got up above the surface, going over the shantytowns that had been built up around the cooling steeples. I flew perfect. I could see the others come out of the droptube behind me, and they were heading off to the strip.

We went for a while. It was raining. There was all of the lights from the factory towers below us, those really hard lights, those bright white ones. They were shining through all the gases, above the tubing and the tanks and ladders. There were cargo ships anchored in the sky. I flew around them, politely, like a gentleman.

We were too angry to speak out loud. Our jaws were like *grrrrrvvvvv*.

So we started to chat.

She was like, *What?*

Nothing.

What nothing?

What nothing what?

She was like, *What are you angry about?*

I breathed, loud and kind of angry. *Why are we going away?*

Because they were making fun of me.

I didn't say anything. I was like, to myself, *This is dumb.* The whole thing was dumb. It was stupid, and it pissed me off.

Violet was pushing me, like, *Well?*

So I, like a shithead, said, *Well, maybe you shouldn't, you know, show off like that.*

Show off? Like what?

Like the way you do sometimes. Using weird words.

I don't use weird words.

Okay. Saying weird shit.

"Oh, screw you!" she yelled out loud. "What do you mean?"

"You know what I mean. It's, like . . . It's something I like about you, but you have to . . . like . . ."

"You like it about me. What is it you like?"

"I like . . . you know, you're so funny, and beautiful, and you . . ."

"Everyone's beautiful. Everyone's pretty as a pansy in a blister pack. That's not what you're talking about."

"You can be a little . . . You can . . . It's kind of scary for people sometimes. It feels . . . It sometimes feels like you're watching us, instead of being us."

"Well, I'm not used to the things you're used to."

"I'm just telling you how it sometimes . . . it feels."

"Thanks for telling me how it feels."

"I'm just telling you."

"Thanks."

We drove on. On *Sky Offenders*, they were having a live thing about drug smugglers getting caught on parasails. There was a lot of static from her chat breaking through. She was pushing it hard.

I dropped my feedwall and let her chat me again.

You think I'm a bitch, don't you?
This is stupid. This is dumb.

She stared out the window.

There's something else wrong, isn't there? I asked her. *Isn't there?*

Nothing. No answer.

For a long time, nothing.

Then I was like, *Is there something else wrong?*

She looked at me. I could tell she was trying not to cry. She said, "Yes."

I was like, *What is it?*

She whispered, "Talk to me. In the air."

I was like biting my lip. I hate these kinds of conversations. I was feeling completely squeam. I went, "Okay. What's, uh, what's wrong?"

For a long time, we went through columns of smoke. They were coming up from below. They were like the rows of trees up the sides of Link's driveway. If we had been happier, I would have done them slalom. They were as gray as, I don't know. They were just gray, okay? The rain hit them.

She said, "My feed is really malfunctioning."

"Right now?"

"I can't feel it right now. But yes."

"Go to a technician."

"I have. I've gone to a bunch. I don't think you . . . Okay, my feed is really, really malfunctioning."

"I don't understand. You told me this already."

"Shut up. I've been going to technicians. The

feedware is starting to produce major errors." She looked scared. She wasn't looking at me. I could feel how much she wasn't looking at me but was looking other places.

"I got my feed later . . . than some kids." She said evenly, "I got my feed really late."

"You told me. So?"

"But the problem is, if you get the feed after you're fully formed, it doesn't fit as snugly. I mean, the feedware. It's more susceptible to malfunction."

"Susceptible?"

"It can break down more easily."

"What does this mean?"

"Nobody knows. The feed is tied in to everything. Your body control, your emotions, your memory. Everything. Sometimes feed errors are fatal. I don't know. I could lose . . . I don't know. They thought it would stabilize. But it didn't. It's getting worse. Meg worse. They told me yesterday it's deteriorating."

"Like rusting?"

"I mean, not the hardware, but the software/wetware interface. They said they didn't . . . I'm not going to cry. I am not going to cry."

I didn't know what I should do. I guessed that I should put my arm around her. I went to move my arm that way. She didn't look very huggable. She was all slouched. She was saying, "They don't know. I could lose my ability to move; I could lose my ability to think. Anything. It's tied in everywhere. They said the limbic system, the motor cortex . . . the hippocampus. They listed all this stuff. If the feed fails too severely, it could interfere with basic processes. My heart could just . . ."

We were sitting there, going through the air. My hands felt really useless. I said, "This sucks. They can't just turn it off? They turned it off before."

"No, they didn't. They disconnected us. They shut down most of the functions. The feed was still on. It's part of the brain."

I looked over at her. She was looking right at me. We were going down the aisle of smoke through the sky. Somewhere over Nebraska, the drug parasailers were being shot out of the air.

She said, "Just drop. Drop and then catch us."

I was staring at the steering column, wondering what the hell she was talking about.

She said, "I want to feel something. Let's feel vertigo together."

That sounded okay to me.

I dropped us.

When we stopped, suddenly both of us had sweat. It was just mainly across our foreheads and fingertips.

She smiled at me. We both felt meg nauseous.

"My fingertips," I said. "They're sweaty."

She nodded.

We flew for a bit. She chatted me like, *Let's go back now. I'm okay.*

No. You don't want to go back, I said. *They were being jerky.*

They weren't being jerky. I was being pretentious.

You weren't—

"I'm fine now."

I said, "We can't just go back. I am like completely—I am—I'm this thing. It's this whole meg thing. I can't go back. Let's go to your house."

"My dad will be there."

"Let's go to my house, then."

"Okay."

With one hand, I changed the course. I held out the other hand. She took it. We flew over gray piles and gray piles and gray piles toward home.

so much
to do

When we got to my house, we went inside and I shut the garage door behind us. We went up the steps and into the family room. We were going to watch something on the feed. We sat there. We weren't really interested in the feed. It was daytime shit, anyway. Soap operas with all these people with the big hair going on crying jags. And lots of puppets. Puppets telling you about every goddamn thing.

"I wish there was someplace we could go," Violet said. "I want to . . . I don't know."

"What do you mean?"

"Just, there's a whole universe out there."

"Yeah."

"I've never been underwater for a really long time."

"I been down on a couple of vacations into the really deep part. It's pretty good. There's a lot of stuff to do."

"I'm just using that as an example," she said, stroking my face.

"You have to have reservations. Otherwise, if you go by yourself, you get the bends."

She was stroking my face and was like, "I probably don't have much time. There's just so much I want to do," which was a difficult thing for her to say, because when she was stroking my face, it looked like it might mean one thing, but on the other hand, it probably meant something else, and it would be embarrassing if it didn't mean what I thought it meant, and if I said something, and then if it turned out that by "so much she wanted to do," she really meant riding trikes across the Sahara.

That would suck.

I said, "Do you mean . . ." I stopped, and tried, "That could be taken to mean that . . . you know . . . we . . ."

My feed was like, *Tongue-tied? Wowed and gaga? For a fistful of pickups tailored extra-specially for this nightmarish scenario, try Cyranofeed, available at rates as low as —*

She was like, "I'm sorry if I embarrassed you at Marty's."

"Would you stop?"

After a minute, I said, "You kept quiet about this for a long time."

She nodded. "A few weeks. I've known."

"You could've told me."

"I could've," she said.

"You didn't need to be thinking about it all alone."

She had her hands in her lap now. She said, "I want to go out and see the world. There's so much. There's . . . just so much."

"Yeah," I said. "Yeah. I don't know. Yeah. This sucks. It meg sucks." I didn't know what to say. We sat there, side by side. We were sitting there, and it seemed like nothing was right. We were done talking.

I held on to her, and she held on to me. We held like that. We were staring at the wall.

She blew out all her breath.

It was a strange moment, like when you get sad after sex, and it feels like it's too late in the afternoon, even if it's morning, or night, and you turn away from the other person, and they turn away from you, and you lie there, and when you turn back toward them, you can both see each other's moles. Usually there seem to be shadows from venetian blinds all across your legs.

She said, "You toss something up in the air, and you expect it to come back down again."

Which made absolutely no sense to me.

We sat and we looked at the fireplace. There

were the fake logs and the fake iron parts. All the bricks were perfect. The walls were all a weird color of white.

Then there was the sound of the front door banging open. Mom was home with Smell Factor. We both were like, *Whoa*.

We pulled apart, and were sitting there. Smell Factor ran into the family room and took off his sneakers one at a time and threw them at the wall. Then he fell down on the rug and phased out and started watching *Top Quark*. Mom was like yelling for him to go pick up his room. He just lay there. She was clapping and calling his name. He just kept up with *Top Quark*. He didn't have it shielded, so we were picking up the whole thing.

Aw, Top Quark, I'll never get the prize at the fair.

Listen up, Down Quark—don't get so down! Remember all your friends are right behind you.

Yeah, Down Quark!

Yeah, we'll sing a song for you! It's a happy, zappy song, full of chuckles and chortles.

Violet ate dinner with us. My father wasn't there, so it went better than the last time. She said some stuff that made my mother laugh. Mom was chatting me about how she was a great girl.

We flew back late at night.

I finally asked her, *Do they know how long?*

No. Earlier, they were saying it could take years.

Now they're not sure. They're saying it will be much faster.

It still could be years.

It's not going to be years. It could happen anytime.

I dropped her off at her house. We didn't make any plans. There weren't any plans.

I spent the rest of the night doing homework. It seemed like that was the only thing left to do.

o   o   o

. . . from *Bow-Wow and Plucky*, on the Christian
      Cyberkidz Network:

*". . . Dad? I keep thinking she'll come back, but I
      know now that she's going to stay away."*

*"Yeah. It's like, it's been so long, I don't know what
      she would look like if she came back, how
      long her hair would be."*

*"She was the best dog. If she came back, it would
      make everything right."*

*"Billy: Nothing will make everything right. That
      dog was a good dog, but she wasn't like a
      superdog, with powers. And I think you'll see
      a little voice inside you that will tell you the
      same."*

*"I still put the suet out by the mailbox, and I still
      sing her my —"*

o   o   o

seashore

We went to the sea, because there wasn't time after School™ to go under it. She and I went to stand beside it. We watched it move around. It was dead, but colorful.

It was blue when the sun hit it one way, and purple when the sun hit it another way, and sometimes yellow or green. We had on suits so we wouldn't smell it.

We sat in the sand. I made an angel with my arms and legs. She piled sand on my stomach. The suits were orange, which was stupid. I hate it when a suit is a really ugly color so you look completely dumb. After she was done piling sand and I was done with my angel, we stared up at the sky.

I was like, *I don't think you have to worry. Science is like, they're always discovering things.*

Yeah. Have you looked at the sea?

You've been reading more of that depressing shit.
Everything's dead. Everything's dying.

Some upcars floated over in the Clouds™. Some cargo ships. Some transit needles, heading off to Norway or Japan or something.

I sat up. I was pissed off with things.

I went, *You know the part that's the really ironic thing? The guy? The hacker? You almost agree with him. He completely fucked you over, and you almost agree with him.*

Yeah, she said. *That's certainly the really ironic thing.*

What? What are you being sarcastic about?

I'm screwed.

See? Like, that's so big negative.

What do you mean? What's positive? My body is completely falling apart. I mean, you saw it with my foot—but it's happening more often. One of my fingers or a part of my face will just freeze up. It's getting more frequent. Like once every other day, for ten or fifteen minutes. Sometimes for a few hours.

Oh shit. Don't tell me this. Oh shit.

And I'm not getting all the images that are supposed to come through on the feed. I'm getting a lot of error messages.

They can fix that.

I don't know. I don't know. I just don't know.

I kicked at the sand. I looked at her. She looked good, through the mask, her big sunglasses brown and purple in the light. I was like, *You know, I . . .*

What?

I really like you.

She hit me on the back of the head. *That'll do,* she said.

○   ○   ○

. . . to Crackdown Alley . . . only on Fox . . .

"Have you given it to her?"

"You can kiss my ass."

"Have you given it to her?"

"What do you think I am?"

"Want me to tell you what I think?"

*"Don't breathe in my face. Go breathe in someone
      else's face."*

"I'll breathe in whatever face I want to breathe in."

"I didn't give it to her."

"What do you think I am?"

"She doesn't have it."

"You can kiss my ass."

"Don't breathe in my face."

"Have you given it to her?"

"Want me to tell you what I think?"

"What do you think I—"

○   ○   ○

182

limbo
and
prayer

On Monday, I went into School™ and I was sitting in homeroom when I saw that Calista had her hair up in this new way, and on the back of her neck was this total insane macrolesion that I never even saw before. I guess I was looking at it kind of *Holy shit!*, because Quendy sat down next to me and chatted, *Impressed? Ain't even real.*

Quendy still hated Calista, because Quendy wanted to be going out with Link herself.

I asked her, *What do you mean?*

Calista got it done yesterday. Quendy made this face. *Now that lesions are "brag." Now that they're the spit.*

It's huge. It's fuckin' huge.

It's not even real. I mean, it's an incision, but it's artificial. It's not even really weeping. Those are beads of latex.

Whoa. I'm surprised her head doesn't, you know, topple off. Like: *badump.*

It's so stupid. God. I can't believe how stupid it is.

Link came in and was kissing Calista on the forehead, with his hand behind her skull, and then he tickled her lesion.

Oh! Unit! I grabbed Quendy's wrist. *Oh, unit, this is like—whoa—total error message. Major system error!*

It's so stupid. I can't believe he's falling for that. It's so dumb.

Whoa! I got to tell Violet about this. She'll go crazy.

Yeah.

She's always looking for like evidence of the decline of civilization.

Yeah.

I looked at Quendy. *What do you mean by that?*

Nothing. Just that Violet is always, like you said. She's always looking for stuff about the decline of civilization, and everything's a mess, da da da.

Is that a problem?

I don't have a problem with it. I think she's nice.

I'm going to chat her about this.

Yeah. Do. She'll think it's funny.

I found a hitch-up to Violet. *You sitting down?* I said. *Calista got an artificial lesion.*

So much for my Frosted Flakes.

Link is tickling her lesion.

Let me just push the bowl toward the wall.

You heard it here first.

Link is . . . He's a great guy, but do you mind if I say he's not the quickest bunny in the centrifuge?

I laughed. *No. Not our Link.*

Did I tell you I thought he was youch the first time I saw him?

Link? Our Link?!? He's butt-ugly. Have you met him?

That's why I thought he was youch. You all were so beautiful. He was hideous. There was some, I don't know, some texture there.

Are you kidding?

Until he opens his mouth.

Right now, he and Marty are skipping rope with some coaxial cable. Ah, he's tripping. He's falling into a desk.

I liked talking to her like this, first thing in the morning. It had a kind of bedroom feel to it. It was kind of flirty, kind of drowsy.

She was like, *Can I ask you a question about Link?*

Yeah?

The name. Link. As in "Missing . . ."?

No, I said.

So?

I don't think you want to know. It won't help much with your worry, you know, about civilization ending and stuff.

Huh? . . . Oh my god. Oh my god. . . . It's a penis thing, isn't it?

No.

Yes, it is. It's some gross boy/locker-room sausage joke, isn't it? Sausage link? Oh. You are so . . . Oh.

No, it's not.

Is so.

Is not. He's the product of this government experiment.

What?

His family's like really old and meg rich? So they got this . . . you know . . .

What?

He was cloned from the bloodstains found on Lucy Todd Lincoln's opera cloak.

There was a long silence.

Then Violet was like, *Mary.*

Yeah. Mary, then. Mary Todd Lincoln.

There was another silence. I sat there, waiting.

She was like, *So he's the genetic clone of Abraham Lincoln.*

Yeah.

Abraham Lincoln.

That's what I said.

Tell me what he's doing now.

Eh . . . the limbo. With the coaxial cable.

I thought so.

Except, he's bending forward instead of backward, so it isn't as hard.

This is extremely grim.

How about over there at your house?

Let me recover.

What's doing at Violet's place?

Dad's off at work. Mom's just a mom-shaped hole in the front door. I'm eating cereal, putting on my stockings, and reading ancient Mayan spells.

You know Mayan?

They're not in Mayan. They're in Spanish. The feed's translating them into English. I'm reading a spell to preserve dying cultures.

Uh-huh.

Written sometime before their empire fell, I guess. "Spirit of the sky, spirit of the earth, grant us descendants for as long as the sun moves, for as long as there is dawn. Grant us green roads; grant us many green paths. May the people be peaceful, very peaceful, and let them not fall; let them not be wounded. Let there be no disgrace, no captivity. O thou Shrouded Glory, Lightning Lord, Lord Jaguar, Mount of Fire, Womb of Heaven, Womb of Earth. Let our people always have days, always have dawns." Then it goes, "O King One-Leg, Giver of Green."

King One-Leg.

Amen, brother.

Link and Marty are doing a lasso with the coaxial cable.

Yeah?

Calista is combing her hair. And she keeps jolting each time she scrapes the edge of the lesion.

Thank goodness for home-schooling.

There's a party on Friday night. You want to come?

Do they hate me?

They don't hate you. Quendy just told me she thought you were nice.

You were talking with her about me.

Don't worry.

I won't. They hate me, don't they?

They think you're like meg cuddly.

Okay. I want to live a little.

Exactly.

I'll come.

Brag.

Will you get me?

Sure.

What time is it right now? Do you have to go?

Yeah. It's time for announcements.

I make my own announcements. Into the garbage can, so it echoes.

Lonely.

I tell myself to come to the office.

Yeah.

Then I pace in circles, waiting for me to show up. I wait and I wait, you know. I wait and I wait in the office, she said, *but me never comes.*

o   o   o

. . . this month's 20 Hot Sex Tips for Girls.

*Hey! You wanna leave your boyf with his head
     spinning? Then check out what Lucia, our
     Lady o' Love, has to say about these chicks
     and their sich in the sack!*

*Natalie from New Jersey messages us, "My guy sez,
     'No nookie at parties!' But I feel that in order
     to do our duty to the party, we gotta—"*

o   o   o

*". . . which is why I ask it. Consider: The United
     States has been instrumental in the overthrow
     of truly genocidal dictatorships. We dole out
     billions of dollars each year in foreign aid. We
     support failing economies. We give harbor to
     many who seek our shores. We are trying to
     do what is right. We are trying to do
     what is—"*

o   o   o

flat hope

On Friday, I went and picked up Violet at her house for the party. I hoped that the party would cheer her up.

I was used to the route, now, and I liked seeing all the stuff I passed, the antennas and chutes and vents, and my feed told me their names as I looked at them—*Charming Lawn Observation Tower; Riverdale Exhaust Hood; Institute for the Study of Psychoeconomy; Bridgeton Playland and Compulsion Center*—and after a while, I knew them by sight, and with each one, I could feel like I was getting closer to Violet, which was like a present which I didn't know what was inside of.

While we flew to the party, she told me about weird things she'd read on the feed, while she was resisting it or whatev. She told me about the scales on butterflies, and the way animals lived in ducts, sometimes whole herds.

People would hear the stampeding through their walls. There were new kinds of fungus, she said, that were making jungles where the cables ran. There were slugs so big a toddler could ride them sidesaddle. "The natural world is so adaptable," she said. "So adaptable you wonder what's natural."

When we got there, people were drinking already and it looked pretty fun. Someone was being a DJ and broadcasting tracks on the feed, so we tuned in, because otherwise you just hear the shuffling while people are moving around with no music on the floor. I have a pretty good auditory-nerve hookup with my feed, so the sound is real spink, and it's good to move to. So we got some drinks and drank them, and said hi to people, and then the feed was going, it was doing this song, *I got some feet, and those feet, they're gonna walk. Walk, feet, you walk, the ten toes, I walk with the feet,* that one, and so we danced to it. It's a kind of low-hips dance, with the draggy elbows, and we did it, it's good for that.

It was all going pretty good until Quendy arrived. When she got there, it was like — *silence . . . wwwwwwwwww (wind) . . . wwwwwwww . . . ping (pin dropping)* — because her whole skin was cut up with these artificial lesions. We were all just looking at her. They were all over her.

She raised her arms. The cuts were like eyes. They got bigger and redder when she moved. "Do you like them?" she said, laughing. "I got it yesterday."

"You're," said Marty, "you're covered with cuts."

"They're not 'cuts,'" she said, smiling like he was an idiot. "First of all, it's the big spit. And second, for your info, it's called 'birching,' and they're lenticels."

Marty and Link were chatting me and each other.

Unit.

Unit.

Whoa, unit.

Violet had her face in her hands.

People were starting to dance again.

I could tell Calista and Loga were chatting up a storm. People were dancing, and the feed was going, *I walk these itty-bitty steps. Away from you. Just itty-bitty steps. I walk away.* Quendy went over to the table with the drinks and poured herself some vodka and Tang. Some other girls were over talking to her.

Violet was standing next to me, like, *I can't believe she did it.*

I went, *It's all for Link. I guess she wanted to outdo Calista.*

Can you even think how much that cost?

I don't know.

Each one of those incisions has to be capped off in plastic.

Yeah. It was probably pretty pricey.

It's the end. It's the end of the civilization. We're going down.

No, it's sure not too attractive. Lenticels.

I just hope my kids don't live to see the last days. The things burning and people living in cellars.

Violet.

The only thing worse than the thought it may all come tumbling down is the thought that we may go on like this forever.

I looked at her. She wasn't joking. Her face was full of lines.

Violet, I said. I took her hands. I had an idea, and I was like, *Let me show you something.*

She didn't say or chat anything. We went away from all the people, up the stairs. The bedroom doors were closed. I took her up past the bedrooms, to the attic. I pulled down the attic, like, the pull, and this ladder folded out. I went up, and willed the light, but there wasn't any feedlink to the light. The light was worked by a string. You pulled it sometimes, and the light went on.

There was all kinds of old shit up there. She came up behind me. When we walked, our footsteps, they were clunky. The boards felt old.

We used to come up here, I said. We played sardines in the closet. You got to hide, and then everyone looks for you, and when they find you, they hide with you. This was this meg good place, because only Link's best friends, we were the only ones that knew about it. We would be up here, all together, and people who weren't his good friends, they'd be walking around downstairs, and we could hear them, and we'd be laughing our asses off.

I used to, when I was hiding here, I kept thinking of when I was littler, you know, younger, before I was good friends with Link. I kept thinking of the time when you're all racing around, and you pass people in the halls, like in cartoons where people go in one door and come out another one. And you're like passing them all and looking in all the laundry places and shit, and it's a big game, and people keep giggling, and then you don't see them again.

Then you're walking around alone. You know, there's this weird moment where you realize that you're alone, and no one else has been walking for a while. You realize that the moment, the exact moment, when you became alone is already over. You've been that way for a while. So you're walking around this empty house, and all the towels are folded up, and the soap is still wet on the soap dish. That's the creepy thing.

She sat down on an old thing.

I kept going. I was like, *You're walking, and everything's empty, but the weirdest thing is that it's not empty at all. The weirdest thing is that you know that you're more alone than anyone, but that more people are thinking about you than ever before. They're all just there, holding their breath, following your, like your every move through the house, listening to your footsteps and the doors opening and closing. So you're more alone, but more watched. It can just go on and on for hours, you walking around, walking on the carpeting, picking up stuff and looking at it, alone, but thought about, until Link gets tired of it, and says the game is over.*

That's exactly it, she chatted.

I didn't know what she meant, but I nodded.

She rubbed her eyes with her palms. I watched her. She stood up and brushed off the butt of her skirt.

She looked around, lifting things up. *What is this junk?*

Old shit, I said. *All this old shit.*

I walked over to one wall. *There are some old pictures.* I lifted them away from the inside of the roof. *Paintings.*

She came to my side. *Whoa.*

We looked at them. Ships at sea. Old-time faces, painted without smiles or anything, dressed in black, holding pieces of paper or big books. Link's dead relatives from long ago. They had old-time names, ones from the past: Abram. Jubilee. Noah. Ezekial. Hope.

Jubilee was frowning. Ezekial was covered with pockmarks.

Hope was this fat old woman with a little dog.

Hope was looking off to the side, as if someone she missed was calling her name.

our duty
to the
party

On the way down, we passed the bedrooms
again. The party had picked up. The doors were
open now, and on some beds, there were people
making out, and on some others, people were
in mal, their legs and arms all twitching and
their heads rocking back and forth, and someone was puking in a roll-top desk and trying to
roll the top down to hide it. Someone's arm was
coming out from under a bed, moving like they
were conducting a symphony orchestra. Violet
walked closer to me, and I put my arm around
her, but her shoulders weren't soft, like she
didn't want to be touched, and we got to the
landing, and heard some kind of smacking
down below, and people cheering.

When we went downstairs, they were all
playing spin-the-bottle like little kids, stretched
out on the floor, swinging their legs. Violet's
back was kind of sagging as she walked down

the stairs in front of me. I was feeling kind of strange, like, I can't really explain it, like as if hypodermics were in the air again, but thrown all ways and still traveling.

Link said, "Hey, take yourselves a seat and play. It's fun."

"It's for kids," said Loga, "but it's kind of sexy?"

Calista was like, "Omigod, it's so uncomfortable sitting on the floor with my lesion. This is so wholly stupid."

Quendy said, "I've only spun once, but I think I did kind of good." She shifted on the floor. Marty's eyes were like meg riveted on her ass, and also on her shoulder blades, where you could see all the red fibers through the splits in the skin. They were shifting as she and this meathead named Ches Something kissed for a turn.

Violet and I sat down. I didn't need to chat her to tell she didn't want to play. We weren't next, which was good, but I really didn't want her to get spun to, because I thought she might get really pissed by the stupidity of the whole game. I was sitting cross-legged, and I put my fist in my cheek and just sat there, telling the bottle with my eyes to keep on going while it spun.

Quendy spun, and got Link, and I was like, *Oh, shit, bad news.* She was really glad. She went over to him, while everyone did this big whoop, and he started to kiss her on the cheek, really just friendly, but she put her palm against his cheek and turned his head so she was kissing him on the mouth, and then put her arms around him. Everyone was completely silent, like *Omigod,* and they kept on kissing, with Link kind of trying to pull back, but being afraid to push too hard, with her cuts everywhere, and Calista staring at them both with this big-hair hatred in her eyes.

Link like tripped and stumbled backward and sat back down next to Calista. Everyone was really uncomfortable, except Marty.

Hey, chatted Marty to the guys, *don't you think Quendy looks good?*

Link was like, *Just shut up and play.*

I was like, *I think it looks stupid.*

It's a good look, Marty chatted, *and kind of fun.*

I was disgusted, like, *Huh? You can see her like muscles and tendons and ligaments and stuff through the lesions.*

Yeah, said Marty, *which makes you kind of think about what's inside, huh? Which is sexy.*

"You must be chatting about how Quendy looks really sexy," said Calista. It was like she was going to start something mean.

"Yeah," said Marty. "We were . . . just saying that the lesions look good."

"Oh," said Quendy. "You like the lesions?"

Link said, "Can we just play?"

"Well, I think they're a lot of fun," Calista said, as if she didn't mean it but meant the opposite.

Link spun again, and while he kissed this other girl, really hardly at all, Calista was still talking to Quendy, saying, in this really mean voice, "And don't let anyone tell you you look stupid."

"Nothing's stupid," said Marty.

"That's right, Quendy," said Calista, "because seeing what's inside of you, all your guts, is just so sexy."

"Calista," said Quendy, trying to stop her, "we're just having fun."

"That's good," said Calista.

The guy Ches Something spun and got Loga. He walked over to her and said, "Time to play."

"Quendy, you know what's fun about your lesions?"

Loga and the Ches guy started kissing, hard. They were playing up their kiss, maybe to like take attention away from the meanness Calista was having. Loga's hands were in Ches's hair, smearing through the hair, her fingers wet with gel.

Calista said, "About your lesions? What's fun is watching a girl who's so desperate for someone's boyfriend that she does something to herself which is really stupid."

There was a quiet part. Then Marty said, "Okay — just — let's — okay — let's — fuckin'— fuckin'—just let's play."

He spun the bottle, and it turned, with the neck flashing, and suddenly I could hear Quendy crying, and then I saw the bottle land on Violet. Marty got up and straightened his pants and walked over.

"Hey, there, sexy," he said. "Let's make this good."

He reached out his hand toward her. She flinched backward. He put his hand on the top of her head.

I said, "This isn't much fun."

"We'll show you fun," said Marty, winking.

"Stop it," said Violet, standing up. "Stop it all."

"What's wrong?" said Marty. He held out his hand toward her wrist. He took her wrist in his hand.

Violet was completely white. She was shaking. Her head, I mean, it was bobbing. She suddenly was yelling, "Can I tell you what I see? Can I tell you? We are hovering in the air while people are starving. This is obvious! Obvious! We're playing games, and our skin is falling off. We're losing it, and we're making out. And you're talking— you're starting to talk in a *fucking sestina! Okay? A sestina! Okay? Stop it! Fuck you! We've got to all stop it!*" She was screaming.

201

People were staring and chatting, and they weren't chatting with me, except Link, who gave me a single, *What's doing with this? Fix it,* before cutting me off.

Violet was screaming, *"Look at us! You don't have the feed! You are feed! You're feed! You're being eaten! You're raised for food! Look at what you've made yourselves!"* She pointed at Quendy, and went, *"She's a monster! A monster! Covered with cuts! She's a creature!"*

And now I was going, "Violet — Don't. Violet! She's not a — she's not a goddamn monster. She's —" but Violet screeched, *"You too! Fuck you too!"* — and she tried to slap me — I grabbed her by the arm — and she tried to scratch at my face, but her hand wasn't working.

She had broken somehow, and she was broken, and, oh fuck, she was sagging and I grabbed her to help her, and she was shaking, and her eyes were all white and rolling around, and she couldn't talk anymore —

— she was choking —

I grabbed her and tried to wrap my arms around her. There was a long line of spit coming out of her mouth. Her legs were pumping up and down. She was broken. She was completely broken.

I was crying and saying to call an ambulance, and people were like, *Fuck no, is she in mal? If she's in mal, no way, we'll get in trouble,* and I was like, *Call a fucking ambulance,* and I tried to do it on my feed, but things were too screwed up, and I could feel the signals going out, and she was breathing again, but she'd gone limp, and I lowered her to the ground, and I put her there, and Quendy was still yelling, "Fuck you!" at her body. "Fuck you!" And Violet was breathing now in heavy, big gasps, but her eyes were closed, and I was leaning next to her asleep body, and squeezing, and squeezing, and squeezing.

I don't know what the others did. There were noises, and women came.

I went with them. And the feed whispered to me about sales, and made all these suggestions about medical lawyers and malpractice, and something happened, and I was sitting beside her in an ambulance, and suddenly I realized, *The party is over.*

The fucking party is over.

Part 4

slumberland

52.9%

The waiting room was white. There were these orbs moving back and forth filled with fluids. They went up and down the halls.

"There will be some delays," said one of the nurses.

She touched her face with her hand. Her pinkie was sticking out. She pressed on her cheek, like she had a toothache.

She said, "Expect a delay."

"Let me tell you a little story," said a woman on a chair next to me.

"He's distressed," said the nurse. She fixed her hair, which was this hair held together with two magic wands. "Breathe deep," the nurse told me. "She's pretty functional."

"What?" I said. "What do you mean?"

"The doctor will talk to you."

"There was this one time," said the woman on the chair.

"When is the doctor coming?" I asked.

"He's here."

"Where?"

"In the room with her."

"But when's he like coming out?"

She sighed. "You might want to rest your yes."

I paced on the floor. The feed was handing me hings. I listened to it, and I paced around, following the pattern of the tiles on the floor.

. . . the poor sales of the Ford Laputa in the Latin American market can't be explained by . . .

. . . craziest prime-time comedy yet. What happens when two normal guys and two normal girls meet in their favorite health-food restaurant? Lots of ABnormal laughs, served with sprouts on the side, is what!

I paced there. I went around all the chairs. I did them slalom. Men locked into giant wheels with their arms and legs spread out were being wheeled past down the hall. People in smocks hit them on the rim to keep them rolling. The wheels rolled by. The people in smocks were whistling. The men in the wheels stared out, their mouths open, their eyes looking at everything flashing by, but the men were not moving at all. Just looking at the world helpless, in circles, the world going by.

Violet's father got there half an hour after I did. I saw him running past me. I didn't wave or anything, because I didn't want to get in the way or be a pain in the butt. People, sometimes, they need to be alone. He went past me and didn't see who I was. That was okay with me. They took him into the room. I waited.

I clapped my hands together softly a bunch of times. I swung my arms at my sides and then clapped. I realized that they were swinging really wide. People were looking up at me. I stopped. I couldn't help a small clap, one last one.

He came out. He was walking real slow. He sat down.

I didn't know whether to talk to him. He was smoothing out the knees of his tribe-suit.

I went over. I said hello, and introduced myself again.

He said, "Oh, yes. Hello. Thank you for . . ."
He was just like, nodding.

"Is she okay?" I asked.

"Yes," he said. "Yes. 'Okay.' Yes, she's 'okay.'"

He didn't seem much like before.

I was like, "What's happening?"

"They're fixing the malfunction. For the time being. The doctor's coming out." His eyes were orange with the light from his feed glasses.

The orbs went past. We waited. Two nurses were talking about the weekend. There was nothing I wanted to watch on the feed. It made me feel tired.

"Can you stop?" said her father to me.

I realized I'd like been clapping again.

"I hate rhythms," he said.

I put my hands down. I stood still, in front of him.

He said, "You can monitor her feed function." He sent me an address. "Go there," he said. "If things neural were going swimmingly with Vi, the number you detect would be about ninety-eight percent."

I went there. It was some kind of medical site. It said *Violet Durn, Feed Efficiency: 87.3%.* He stared at me. I stared at him. We were like, just, there. The efficiency went up to 87.4%. He turned his head. Someone was whistling two notes in the hallway.

Violet was not a bitch. She didn't mean those things. It was because of the damage. It was making her not herself. I told myself that again and again.

But it didn't matter if she was right or wrong about what she said. It was the fact she said it, especially to Quendy, calling her a monster, screaming like one of those girls in black at school, the ones who sat on the floor in the basement and talked about the earth, the ones who got rivets through their eyes just to make people think they were hard. I wanted Violet to be uninsane again, just a person who would touch my face.

"She's awake," said a nurse. "Please come in."

She wanted him. Not me. I just stood there. He turned around and went in.

After a while, he came out and sat down again.

The nurse said, "Now you."

I followed her in.

Violet was sitting in a floating chair with lots of cables. Some of them went to her head.

When I came in, she looked away from me.

"I'm sorry," she said.

We stood that way for a little while. She was dressed in just a gown again. Like when we were getting to know each other, back on the moon.

She said, "I said I'm sorry."

I didn't want to piss her off, so I figured what she wanted me to say, and I said, "I'm just . . . I'm worrying about you."

She shrugged. I watched her. I didn't know how close she was to the person who had gone completely fugue at the party.

I asked, "How did they say you are?"

"Fine," she said. "For a little while." She held on to her kneecap. She moved it back and forth.

"How long?" I asked.

She didn't answer.

I said, "You don't have to say."

"Not long."

She looked up at me. She was almost crying.

She was like, *I can't even say everything I need to say.*

Don't be — don't — it's all going to be good.

She rubbed her eye. *Why are you standing so far away?*

I was like, *You're covered with cables.*

She was like, *Oh. Yeah. Yeah.*

We were just like standing there for a minute. Well, she was sitting, but I was standing. I looked up at her. She was moving her kneecap again. I patted myself on my hips. It was like, *Tip-tip-a-tip-tip. Tip tap.*

She went, *It's funny that you can move your kneecap all around with your fingers, but you couldn't move it with your muscles if you tried.*

One of the orbs came in and started to circle around her.

I said I had to go.

She said she'd see me later.

I said my upcar was back at Link's. I'd forgot.

She said I should go and get it.

I said I hoped she was okay.

She said she was pretty okay. She'd chat me later. Was that okay? Could she chat me?

I was like, *Oh, sure. Sure.*

No. Really?

Sure. Yeah. On the chat.

I nodded. Finally I waved, kind of pathetic, and I went out. The orb was in front of her face. I couldn't see what she looked like. I went out into the hall.

Later, my mom came and picked me up, and we went and got my upcar. The others weren't there at Link's house anymore. Link was in the back, by his pool. He waved, and yelled over to me, "She okay?" I chatted him yes, and he chatted me that that was good, and I got in my upcar and flew home behind my mom.

We had bean cubes and fish sticks for dinner. I had a couple of helpings. There was still time to do my homework, but I watched the feed instead. Some cops found a bunch of rods in a warehouse and were trying to figure out what they were. Durgin, the star of the show, said they belonged

213

to a pimp. His assistant had a run in her stockings. She bent down to fix it. Later I went to bed. I couldn't get to sleep. My parents had turned off the sun hours before. The light outside the blinds was just gray.

Finally, I guess I must have fell sleep. At least, I dreamed, and there were beads of water going along some string, and Violet said, "How many do you need before you're done?" and I said, "These are yours, first," and she said, "How many do you need?" and I said, "You know. You completely know," and she said, "That's why I want to hear it from your mouth."

87.1%

The next day, I was at her house. It was all weird. We didn't talk. I don't know why. We didn't open our mouths. We just sat there, silent, chatting.

It's not you, I argued. *It's the feed thing. You're not like that.*

Maybe I am like that. Maybe that's what's wrong.

She rubbed her hands together. *I'm sorry. Please. Tell Quendy I'm sorry.*

Her father was walking down the stairs near us. We could hear him through the wall.

She chatted, *I lost a year of my memories.*

I didn't understand, first. *What?*

I lost a year. During the seizure. I can't remember anything from the year before I got the feed. When I was six. The information is just gone. There's nothing there.

She was pressing her palms into her thighs as hard as she could. She watched herself real careful like it was a crafts project. She went, *Nothing. No smells. No talking. No pictures. For a whole year. All gone.*

I just looked at her face. There were lines on it I hadn't seen before. She looked sick, like her mouth would taste like the hospital. She saw me looking at her.

She was like, *Don't worry, Titus. We're still together. No matter what, we'll still be together.*

Oh, I went. *Yeah.*

She reached out and rubbed my hand. *I'll remember you. I'll hold on to you.*

Oh, I chatted. *Okay.*

She went, *God, there's so much I need to do. Oh my god. You can't even know. I want to go out right now and start. I want to dance. You know? That's this dumbass thing, because it's so cliché, but that's what I see myself doing. I want to dance with like a whole lacrosse team, maybe with them holding me up on a Formica tabletop. I can't even tell you. I want to do the things that show you're alive. I want to eat huge meals with wine. I want to go to the zoo with you.*

Zoos suck, I said. *All the animals just sit there and play with their toes.*

I want to go on rides. The flume, the teacups, the Tilt-a-Whirl? You know, a big bunch of us on the teacups, with you and me crushed together from the centrifugal force.

I wasn't really wanting to think about us crushed together right then, or about us in a big group, where she might go insane again, so I just looked like, *Yeah. The teacups!*

And she was still saying, *I want to see things grazing through field glasses. I want to go someplace now. I want to get the hell out of here and visit some Mayan temples. I want you to take my picture next to the sacrificial stone. You know? I want to run down to the beach, I mean, a beach where you can go in the water. I want to have a splashing fight.*

I just sat there. Her father was working on something in the basement. It sounded like he had some power tools. Maybe he was drilling, or like, cutting or boring.

She went, *They're all sitcom openers.*

What?

Everything I think of when I think of really living, living to the full—all my ideas are just the opening credits of sitcoms. See what I mean? My idea of life, it's what happens when they're rolling the credits. My god. What am I, without the feed? It's all from the feed credits. My idea of real life. You know? Oh, you and I share a snow cone at the park. Oh, funny, it's dribbling down your chin. I wipe it off with my elbow. "Also starring Lurna Ginty as Violet." Oh, happy day! Now we go jump in the

217

fountain! We come out of the tunnel of love! We run through the merry-go-round. You're checking the park with a metal detector! I'm checking the park with a Geiger counter! We wave to the camera!

Except the Mayan ruin.

What about it?

There aren't, I like pointed out, *there aren't the sacrificial stones. In sitcoms.*

No, she said. *That's right. Chalk one up for the home team.*

We sat. She fixed her hair with her hand.

I asked her, *What did it feel like? At the party?*

She waited. Then, she admitted, *It felt good. Really good, just to scream finally. I felt like I was singing a hit single. But in Hell.*

Later, before I left, I watched Violet and her father petition FeedTech for free repairs. Violet's dad couldn't pay for all the tests and shit himself. None of it was covered by medical, because the feed wasn't medical.

They sent a message to FeedTech explaining what happened. I sat there while they spoke it together. It was all about how she had lost her memory, and how sometimes she couldn't move parts of her, and about how she had gone completely fugue-state. They asked FeedTech to take on payments for research and repairs. They said that FeedTech had to, because it was about the life of a girl.

Her feed's warranty had expired years ago.

"We will present this petition to several corporate sponsors," said Violet's dad. "If you do not acquiesce, others will. We will find someone who will support this repair. We will take our business elsewhere."

"Please," said Violet. "We need your financial assistance."

"If you want us as customers," said her father.

They sent the message. After that, we didn't say much.

Quendy and I talked the next day. We were sitting on big cubes, they were made of concrete. We sat side by side.

I was like, "She's really sorry."

Quendy nodded. She still had the lesions all over her. When she moved her head, I could see a lesion on her neck open and close like a fish mouth singing a country song.

Quendy said, "I was like . . . I can't go out in public anymore. At first, I was so living eternally in a tool shed. But Loga was like really, really good? She was sitting with me that night. We went back and sat around at my house. She was like, *Da da da, she was completely in mal, don't listen to her, da da da, she's a complete fuguing bitch.*"

"She's—but she's not—"

"I know. That was just what I like needed to hear then."

"She feels real bad."

"I know. It wasn't her."

I didn't say anything. I just nodded. Quendy brushed her hair back out of her face. I rubbed the corner of the concrete with my thumb.

Quendy asked, "She okay?"

I shook my head. "She's scared. They say that it's . . . The feed isn't working well with her brain anymore."

"Omigod." She looked at me. "What does that mean?"

"I don't know. The whole brain is tied in to the feed. The whole brain, like the memory and the part that makes you move and the part for your emotions."

"The limbic system."

"I don't know."

"I just looked it up."

"Okay."

"There's a diagram." She sent me the site.

"Okay." I sat there.

"Maybe you should check it out," she said, a little angry. "It'll help you understand what's happening to her."

I pulled up my leg and untied and tied my shoe.

"Don't you want to know?"

I said, "I guess not."

"You know," said Quendy, "this isn't re: the

world serving you some meg three-course dump banquet. It isn't re: the world serving me some dump banquet. She's the one who this is happening to. I don't know what you're saying to her? But I hope you aren't sulking weirdly."

She looked over at me. I just sat there.

She added, "Making her feel low-grade."

She put her hand on my leg.

"Hey," she said. "Hey."

Through the holes in her hand, the blood in her veins was blue.

When I woke up the next morning, there was a message from Violet waiting in my cache.

It's three-fifteen in the morning, she said. *I haven't heard anything from FeedTech. I'm lying here. You're probably sound asleep right now. I like to picture you asleep. You have beautiful lips.*

My mom never had the feed. She didn't get it installed when she was little. Her parents said they were going to wait until she was old enough to understand and make her own decision about it, like Catholic confirmation. She decided not to have the feed installed. She called it "the brain mole."

My father's family didn't have the money to buy feeds for my dad and my uncle. The feeds were newer then, and they were more expensive. They were advertised with these silver see-through heads with the chip inside them. The heads would be spinning around at the mall, with the mouths of the heads calling your name.

My mom and dad both went through college without the feed. I guess it was really hard. They couldn't remember things the way everyone else could, or see the models that were in the air, you know, of chromosomes or stamens. But they both went on to grad school. That's where they met.

I always thought it was strange that they decided to have a kid at a conceptionarium. I guess they really wanted to have me freestyle. They talked about it a lot. Well, I mean, they'd only been going out for a few months, but, you know, a lot for that. Anyway, the ambient radiation was already too bad by then for freestyle. So they went test-tube.

I think my first memory of my mom is her carrying me on her shoulders through the mall. She would constantly be whispering jokes to me, little jokes between the two of us. She especially made fun of plastic. She'd say, "They're all wearing oil. All their clothes. They don't have anything on but oil." I would whisper back to her, "They're wearing dinosaurs. Dead dinosaurs drippy all over them." She would whisper, "Trilobites." I would whisper, "Old plants." She would whisper, "It's the height of fashion." And I would say, "Missus — missus lady — those are some nice old plankton."

For an hour and a half today, I couldn't move my leg. My toes were clenched. My knee was all locked up. I didn't chat you. I didn't want to worry you. You don't talk much now. I went to a technician. By the time I waited, the leg started to work again. My dad was there with me. He's not doing very well. I can't feel anything wrong with the leg now. I'm lying here in bed, lifting it up and down. It seems fine. Except it's kind of cramped from the clenching.

I'm looking up at my leg. I'm moving my toes, squelching them. That's a great feeling, squelching, like in mud. Do you know, mud? When it's in your yard? And you know the day's going to get hot again when the rain's over, because that's what the neighborhood association has decided? So you can just stand there, and wait for the sun?

And it's your one time on Earth, I mean, your hundred years, that's all you have, so there you are, on Earth, a little kid, the one time you'll be a little kid, and you're standing, waiting for the artificial sun, and feeling the mud, and at that point, your toes still work perfectly. So you stand there, and you squelch your toes, and you raise your arms up above your head, and you watch the clouds get sucked back into ducts in the sky. And that's it. That's an afternoon.

That's all.

I hope you're okay this morning, too.

82.4%

I didn't listen to all of it immediately. I was lying there in bed. I saw that it was going to be long, and I stopped after a few sentences. There was a smell like the hospital. It was like sickness. At first, I thought it was an attachment, but it wasn't. It was coming from my nose. I got up and took my shower, and I got dressed and went downstairs and had one of my dad's Granola Squeezes, and went out to my upcar and started to drive to School™.

I listened to the rest while the upcar drove me.

When the upcar settled in the School™ parking lot, I kept staring out the front window. I didn't want to get out. Kids were running everywhere and pushing each other. Their backpacks were all sparkly in the sun.

I could still smell the hospital in my nose. It wasn't anything around me. It was her. I stopped breathing, but the smell was still there. I held my breath.

I stared out the window at the School™. Everyone went in through the doors. The leaves on the trees turned red to show I was late. My hand was still on the lift shift. I just left it there, in some weird kind of trance, as if I was waiting there for the right moment to pull back, drop anchor, and fall upward into the sky.

80.9%

Definitive list of things I want to do:

1. *Dancing.*
2. *Fly over an active volcano. Spit stuff into magma.*
3. *Could the dancing be in a nightclub with lots of mirrors? And people wear tuxedos, and there's a big band, and perhaps some mob activity? And you'll keep staring at a cigarette girl named Belinda, from Oklahoma, and I'll say, "Damn you, man—damn you—can't you keep your eyes in your sockets like everyone else?"*
4. *I want to sit with you in a place where I can't hear engines.*
5. *Is there any moss anywhere?*
6. *I want to go under the sea and watch the last fishes. I want to sit in one of those bubbles in the middle of a school.*

7. *I want to see art. Like, I want to remind myself about the Dutch. I want to remind myself that they wore clothes and armor. That some of them fell in love while they were sitting near maps or tapestries.*

8. *I want to go up into the mountains with you for a weekend. Where people don't usually go.*

9. *When we're there, I want to go to a store that sells only beer and jerky.*

10. *I want to rent a hotel room with you. As Mister and Missus Smith.*

11. *I want to say we're from Fort Wayne. And have the proprietor frown, and know we're lying, but still nod.*

12. *I would like to actually be from Fort Wayne. Or from a small town outside of it. We won't have the feed, and we'll go to "movies" on dates. We'll kiss in the upcar. And then, when I'm in my twenties, I'll go east to the big city, to find my first job. And have people at parties sitting on the arms of chairs, drinking wine out of plastic cups. People with strange haircuts, things sheared into geometrical shapes.*

13. *And I want to go into "the office" every day, sometimes even on weekends, in some kind of suit, and be someone's administrative assistant, and complain to you through the*

feed while I'm at my desk about my bitch of a manager or my pervert boss. You'll be my boyfriend from home. You're also from Fort Wayne.

14. *I want to get older.*
15. *I want to see the years pass.*
16. *Sometime, I want to wear a cardigan and have a golden retriever named . . . I don't know. I guess named after someone obscure—usually, isn't that how it goes for people like me? Their cats are named like Tutankhamen or Mithridates. Their dogs are named for great thinkers, like Jefferson or Socrates or Thomas Paine. I guess I'll call mine Paine.*
17. *I want famous artists and composers to come and stay at my house. You know, someone named Gerblich who's writing a piece where you take an ax to the piano.*
18. *My grandkids will come up to see me when I'm in my cardigan. I want them to call me Nana. We'll sit by the lake, which won't steam like lakes do and won't move when the wind isn't on it, or burn sticks. I'll tell them about their great-grandparents, and show them old pictures on the family site. I'll tell them how their great-great-great-grandfather fled Germany just before the Second World War. He was a homosexual,*

and had to wear a pink triangle on his arm. He got to America and married a pretty Marxist candy striper to get citizenship, and eventually they decided to have kids. My grandkids will ask me what a candy striper is.

19. When we make dinner, little Shirley will help me shuck the corn.

20. I want to tell her about what her mama used to do when she was just hatched, the silly things Mama did when she was a child.

21. I'll lean on the sink, and I won't remember the hours spent in waiting rooms, the doctors touching me with metal rods, pushing me back onto gurneys, the technicians having secret conferences with my father. I won't remember what it is like to stare at my leg and press it with my fingernails until the skin turns white, and then red, and then blue, and still not have any feeling. I won't remember what's really going to happen, that nerve-silence spreading over the whole of my body, like a purple cloud, that emptiness, that inactivity. I won't remember watching you stand by my bed when I can't move, watching you staring down; I won't remember you apologizing for not coming sooner; I won't remember you standing there bored by my bedside as I slur words,

standing there waiting to feel like you've stayed long enough so that you're a good person and you're allowed to leave. I won't remember any of that, because it won't happen. I'll lean on the sink, and my granddaughter will cut paper molecules with her scissors for a project for school.

22. I'll go out and call for the dog, because it's getting to be evening, and there are coyotes out there in the woods. The night will be falling. By the screen door, I'll call— "Paine!" And the trees will rustle. "Paine! Paine!" And he'll come when I call.

78.6%

I was staring at a girl's sweater. I couldn't like focus on the teacher. The teacher was a hologram that day. There had been some funding cuts. The school band was gone, and so were the alive teachers.

I didn't send a message back to Violet. I didn't even listen to her list all the way through the first time. I skimmed it. I fast-forwarded it. Then, like each hour or so, I'd go back, and I'd listen to one part of it.

When I got to the end, that was it.

I stared at the back of the girl in front of me.

With a hologram, like when your teacher is one of them, if you aren't looking right at them, they sometimes seem to be hollow. You see them and suddenly they don't have a face that pokes out. Their face pokes in, their nose and so on, and there is nothing inside them.

If you don't look right at them, they can look just like an empty shell.

77.8%

Hey, she chatted. What's doing? I wish I was with you today. I always wish I was with you. . . . Oh, did you get my list? Titus? . . . Titus?

76.3%

After School™ that day I went over to Link's with Marty and Link. We were sitting outside near the pool. Link asked me about Violet, and how she was doing. I said I guessed she was okay. He asked me hadn't I talked to her. I said I hadn't, not for a couple of days.

She had tried chatting me a few times since she sent me the list, but I had on my busy signal.

We sat there for a while, and Link and Marty went swimming, and we played water volleyball, which was hard with three people. So we stood there for a minute, until I said, "Does anyone else want to go in mal?"

They looked at me. They were like, *Unit*. Marty said sure, and Link said he had a tip for this great new site.

They went, "You sure?"

I was like, "What I say?"

They nodded.

We got out of the pool and dried off with towels. We went inside. We found the site. It had these meg-ass warnings all over it, it was Swedish. We all clicked on it and we could feel it tap our credit, and then suddenly it hit me all at once. It was colored bricks, first, and I fell down because they were coming too quick. Then I could start to see the bottom of the sofa. Link was crawling, and his face was taken up by it. It kept coming in wave after wave. The floor was steep. I held on to the lamp but it dumped me.

The static was covering everything and so when we went somewhere, I couldn't even see where we were going. I just watched the others. From the static, I could see their mouths talking. Violet asked me what was going on with me. I tried sitting up and answering but she wasn't in the room. That was funny and I laughed.

Marty thought I was laughing at something else, so he got started, too, and pretty soon we were all laughing, and so everybody at the ice-cream store was looking at us. We'd just bought a tub and I was like, *If I eat this I'm going to puke,* and Marty went, *Unit, how the fuck did we get to an ice-cream store anyway?* and I was like, *Whoa, unit, shit, I hope you didn't drive.* Some parents were moving their kids away from us, and Link went to them, "Boo! Okay? BOO!" He spread his hands. There was light coming from his fingers. I

pointed and said, "Light." Marty said, "Bright."
Link said, "Sight." Marty said, "Night." I said,
"Kite." Link said, "Have you ever thought about
how a kite is held up by nothing?" Marty said it
wasn't nothing, fuckhead, it was air. Like, air.
Like, as in fuckin' air. Air.

We went out into the main part of the mall
and went into a music store but it was really
really really loud, so we went out? And we went
down to a clothes store, and sat in the dressing
room for a while. It was quiet there, except the
banging on the door and asking us to leave. I
showed Marty and Link the message from Violet
with the list, the things she wanted to do before
she died, and they read it, and Marty said, *Fuck,
unit, fuck,* and Link said, *Whoa, that's intense, she's
one weird bitch.* I said she wasn't a bitch and he
said that that's not what he meant, that's just what
he said. Marty asked me why I wasn't talking to
her, and I said I was talking to her, I just hadn't.
He said that message was so fuckin' sad it made
him want to like fuckin', you know, bawl his eyes
out, and I said, *Do you think she's being mean to
me? In telling me about that part with me standing
by her bed?* They said, *Mean how?* And there kept
on being this stupid banging on the door, which
woke me up several times in one minute. I was
curled up in this ball, like doing a cannonball,
but on carpeting, with my arms wrapped around

my leg. There were some pants hanging on one of the hooks. We checked a few times, but we all had our pants on, so they must have belonged to the lady who left just before we came in. We thought it was funny that she hadn't come back for them, and we laughed about that. It was good to be with friends. Violet asked me again what was going on, and I told her to shut the fuck up, but luckily, I told her that out loud, and she wasn't there, but chatting.

We got up and opened the door, and there was this kid dressed in perfect clothes, like, with doughnut rings on his arms, and he asked us would we please leave as we appeared to be under the influence.

We went out and sat near the fountain, watching the water, which was interesting, because your vision slowed it down so much that you could see each individual droplet, which was fascinating, each one of them, falling down, and making a ring in the water, and that ring spreading with all of its tentacles reaching up and then dropping back, and then the water rocking. Violet asked me what I was doing, was I out of School™ yet.

Unit, I said. *I'm way out of School™.*

She was like, *How are you? I haven't heard from you for days.*

Violet, I was like, *Violet. Violet. Violet.*

Hey. What's up?

Violet. Violet. Violet.

Are you in mal?

I'm coming over.

Hey. Yoo-hoo. Hey. Stop.

I can't remember if my upcar's here.

Don't fly like this. You're slammed. Have you heard about this Central American stuff? Two villages on the Gulf of Mexico, fifteen hundred people—they've just been found dead, covered in this black stuff.

"Gentlemen," I said to the other two. "I got to go."

Have you heard about it? This is big. It seems like an industrial disaster. The Global Alliance is blaming the U.S.

"I am hoping, sirs, that we brought separate vehicles for . . ." I said. "Things. Vehicles."

Don't fly right now, she said. *Don't fly. You're meg jazzed.*

No, I'm not.

You're spewing a substream of junk characters all over the place. You're completely unformatted. What are you doing? Why did you do this? Just stay there.

I'm at the mall. In mal. At the mall. In mal. At the mall.

Oh. Oh, god. Don't do anything. Wait for it to wear down.

I'm coming to see you. I feel. I feel bad.

You are such a shithead. You don't know what happened to me this morning. And the news. Titus—this morning . . . I can't believe in the middle of all this, you went and got malfunctioned. You are such an asshole and a shithead.

"On level three," said Marty, who I discovered was still sitting in front of me. "Of the parking lot. Next to mine. You okay to drive?"

"I'll do it autopilot," I said.

"You sure?"

I said, "The horse knows the way to carry the sleigh, through the . . ." I scratched my hair.

Marty nodded. Link started singing "Ho, Ho, Elflings, Santa's on His Way," which was the completely wrong song.

I went up to the parking lot. I looked for level three. The in mal was starting to wear off a little. It was mainly just euphoria now. I found my upcar next to Marty's. Marty's upcar was kind of touched and wrinkled by a pillar.

I flew. Once I got up the droptube, I put the upcar in autopilot. I was almost asleep. I dreamed about sweater vests, mainly. *Spreadable cheese! But with a difference!*

. . . after the Prime Minister of the Global Alliance issued a statement that, quote, "the physical and biological integrity of the earth relies at this point upon the dismantling of American-based

corporate entities, whatever the cost." It is thought that the American annexation of the moon as the fifty-first state . . .

Into her droptube, and it found its way to her level, which was on the bottom, or maybe just toward the bottom, her suburb was.

I flew to her street. She was waiting outside her house. She had her hair up in this really nice way. I pulled up in her driveway and left the upcar hovering. I opened the door and stumbled to hang out of it.

I was like, "Unette."

"Don't go inside. My dad will know."

"Big unsteady. Biiiiig unsteady."

"You are such a shithead. Okay. Get down from there. Let's spend some time on the lawn."

I climbed down. I had to touch the grass with my heel like all these times to make sure it was still hard. She took my hand.

"Your list," I said. "It will just take about five days."

"What?"

"Look at your list. It will just take about five days. I mean, for us to do everything. Well, okay, the list before the part, you know, where you become from Fort Worth."

"Fort Wayne. Activity twelve."

"Huh?"

"Activity twelve. Actually being from Fort Wayne."

"Activity twelve is out of the question."

"I'm glad you came back. I was worried you weren't going to."

"We're going to do it all, unette. We're going to find the mountains."

"Hey. Hey. Calm down. Have you heard the news? It's awful."

"I think maybe if I sleep again, we can start by going dancing. We better wait for the weekend to go to the mountains. I have School™. You don't."

"No. I just have mourning."

"What?"

"My father sitting around, staring at me. He's stopped teaching me. He says he'll tell me whatever I want to know, but that there's no reason for lessons anymore."

I felt like what she was telling me was real important, but the trees were so green, and I could smell the grass near my face. She told me that her father asked her what she wanted to know, and she asked him whether there was a soul, but I just put my face against the ground, and the dirt was cool, and the grass was tickling my nose, and I fell asleep, and heard the news talking through my eyes.

76.2%

While I slept on her lawn, she sent me a message. *This is from earlier today,* it said. *The FeedTech response. Check out the attachment.*

It was a full feed-sim of Violet's sensations. It explained a lot. It was memories from that morning. I tried them on.

I was Violet, walking down the stairs in her house. There was a poster next to me with a picture of an Asian lady holding up an old machine. I was whistling some stupid bore-core tune. I took the steps two at a time.

Suddenly, I couldn't move my legs, I couldn't even scream, I just tried to grab on to the banister. I was falling backward. I hit the walls with my hand as hard as possible and then my face hit the carpet on the stair and I was sliding down on my butt. The rug on each stair was burning the side of my face, it was like underwater.

There was no space in me for breathing.

I lifted my head up and dropped it. I was lying on the floor of the downstairs. It was dark because I hadn't turned on the light. I was trying to breathe.

Trying to breathe.

That was when Nina appeared.

I clutched at the air.

She chatted, *Hi, I'm Nina, your FeedTech customer assistance representative. Have you noticed panic can lead to big-time underarm odor? A lot of girls do. No sweat! Why not check out the brag collection of perspiration-control devices at the DVS Superpharmacy Hypersite? But that's not why I'm here, Violet.*

First little breaths, then bigger ones, then finally I could feel my face and my back hurting, and I had my wind back. My legs were in funny places and I couldn't feel them at all.

Nina said, *I'm here to inform you that FeedTech Corp has decided to turn down your petition for complimentary feed repair and/or replacement.*

"No," said Violet/me out loud. "No, fuck you. Please. Please. No."

We have also tried to interest other corporate investors in your case.

Violet was like, *Please. Please. I need help.* We couldn't move our legs. We were lying there, and we couldn't move them, and Nina was saying, *We tried our best to interest a variety of possible corporate sponsors, but we regret to tell you that you were turned down.*

What? Why?

We're sorry, Violet Durn. Unfortunately, FeedTech and other investors reviewed your purchasing history, and we don't feel that you would be a reliable investment at this time. No one could get what we call a "handle" on your shopping habits, like for example you asking for information about all those wow and brag products and then never buying anything. We have to inform you that our corporate investors were like, "What's doing with this?" Sorry—I'm afraid you'll just have to work with your feed the way it is.

Violet lay back down in the dark, her legs starting to sting. She called out loud for her dad. She was sobbing.

Maybe, Violet, if we check out some of the great bargains available to you through the feednet over the next six months, we might be able to create a consumer portrait of you that would interest our investment team. How 'bout it, Violet Durn? Just us, you and me—girls together! Shop till you stop and drop!

Go away, Violet said in a burst over the feed. *Go away. Go—away.*

Nina smiled. *I've got a galaxy of super products we can try together!*

Please. I'm alone in the house and I fell down. Please go away. Please don't help.

That's where Violet clipped off the end of her memory when she sent it to me. Her, lying in the dark, on the ground, in the basement, waiting for her father to come and help.

Feeling the pain in her head. Wondering if it was just from falling, or if it was the feed rusting somehow, as if she could feel it, rusting brown in her brain.

When I woke up, I had a headache. We didn't go dancing. It was already getting dark in her neighborhood, and her father was staring out the window at her, and I felt like a jerk, because it was pretty clear he was thinking, *My daughter is spending these last like precious hours with some malfunctioned asshole.*

She was sitting next to me on the grass. Upcars were shooting over, back and forth, people were commuting. It was the end of the day.

She asked whether I wanted to stay for dinner, and I was feeling bad about coming over and embarrassing her, so I said no. The feed was trying to mop up my headache. I could feel it doing nerve blocks. There was a message in my inbox from Sweden saying they hoped I had enjoyed Cow-kicker, please come again. There was no way I was trying that shit again, because it had a mean attack and a bastard of a decay. I felt awful.

We sat on the grass.

I was like, "I didn't mean . . . I didn't know that they had sent you that. The refusal. I didn't know."

"You didn't ask."

I kept being silent so she could bring stuff up, if she wanted to. She didn't bring any of it up. She just talked about music, and told me about some concerts she'd been to, a few years before. She didn't like fun music, but sarcastic music like bore-core.

I kept waiting for something to happen. I wanted her to do something, like grab my hand.

Her father watched us through the window, with his lips pursed.

After a while, I started to want her to grab my hand so much that I put it on the grass right next to her hip. She kept talking about Diatribe on tour. It was like we weren't going out. I felt like I wanted to bump up against her accidentally, so we'd touch. But I wasn't going to touch her if she didn't touch me first.

We stopped talking, and she asked if I had to go. I said I probably should, because it was a long ride to get home. She asked if I felt better, and I said I couldn't feel anything.

I stood up and looked in the window at her

father. He was sitting with his elbows on his knees, staring at the bottom of a garbage can. Violet walked me out to the upcar. I waited near it for her to try to kiss me. She didn't, so I said good-bye, and crawled in.

She looked at me, and started to smile. She raised her hand.

I closed the door.

I lifted off.

The next day, her arms stopped working for an hour, and she panicked and had to be given a sedative.

59.3%

That night I could feel another message caching. It was a big one. It was huge. It started, *It's three again. I'm awake. I've been listening to requiems, and ordering more. I've been listening to burial rites from all over the world.*

Some places they dance and chant. Some places they tear their clothes. Some places they play choirs of bamboo clarinets. Some places they scream. In Polynesia, they wail, but the wailing is close to a song. It's strange—once you start listening to wailing that's also singing, that's also like a ritual, you start to wonder—how much does anyone really miss anyone else? How much are they just crying because it's what they have to do, the song they have to sing? Some Australian women have to fall silent when they're grieving—it's required—and they speak for the rest of their lives only with their hands.

Titus, I'm afraid of silence. I'm afraid my memory will go soon. When I try to think about that year that disappeared, from six to seven, it's nothing. I mean, I can't remember anything. I can remember remembering, but I can't remember anything that happened to me right before I got the feed. I'm afraid I'm going to lose my past. Who are we, if we don't have a past?

So I'm going to tell you some things. Especially the things before I got the feed. You're the most important person in my life. I'm going to tell you everything. Some day, I might want you to tell it back to me.

She kept sending things. I didn't open them. I let them sit. I was walking around School™ the next day, feeling them like, feeling them crowd me. It was like something was always spilling. It was always there.

I went home that afternoon. In the upcar, I was afraid I would look at the memories. They were getting bigger. She was sending them every few minutes. Sometimes, something would bleed through — her father, younger, throwing her a baseball. Her mother, wearing sandals and a proton lid. The smell of some sauce cooking. Stories she told, from before she got the feed. I would get a few words, something about an aunt, or a camel, or a guitar, or some shit.

I didn't listen to any of them, any of the stories. I just kept them. I didn't touch them on the way home. They just bled.

I got home. I had a headache. I told the feed to shut off the headache. It sent me a message about how much I was caching, and asked if I wanted to open it.

I sat down at the table, and then walked around. She was bombarding me.

Finally, I got a message that she'd stopped. My lines were clear.

I went to the kitchen to get a drink of water. I filled a glass. I looked at the window over the sink.

I deleted everything she had sent me.

I went into the living room and sat on the sofa. I didn't feel good.

I sat on the sofa. I looked at the fireplace. I had deleted all her memories.

Later on, she chatted me, saying, *What's your answer about the weekend idea? We'll have to sneak around my dad, because he doesn't want me to see you—but don't worry—don't worry. We'll be together, whatever happens.*

I didn't know what weekend idea she was talking about, so I didn't answer her.

The walls of my room were all white. They had hotspots, where if you looked at them, posters would appear, but I shut them off. There was nothing on my walls.

I didn't do my homework.
I went to bed.
I lied there, face up.
I didn't sleep.

57.2%

I couldn't think on Friday night, because Smell Factor was crying and running around the house throwing things. My dad hadn't been home for a few weeks, and my mom was really angry and kept yelling at Smell Factor, and he kept running all up and down the carpets. He was directing these like blasts of kids' programs in different directions so it hurt to walk around because you kept getting caught in his beams, like,

IS YOUR HEAD A SQUARE? POINT TO ONE NOW!

. . . CHUCKIE, HAVE YOU LOST YOUR SOCKS . . . AGAIN?!?

. . . Or suddenly you're like doubling over, and it's

. . . ROBOT PALS YOU CAN KEEP IN YOUR HAIR! SIX TO A PACKAGE, GIVE MOM A SCARE! ("Wow!" "Meg brag!" "Mine's called Looty!")

I was staying in my room to avoid having my like brain blown up by Smell Factor's broadcasts. I heard Mom running after him, telling him she'd give him some cookie dough if he'd stop. I sat there and wondered what to do, because I was bored of the games I had, and it was just Friday, but I didn't know if anyone was going out, or what we were supposed to do that weekend.

Mom called up to me, "Hey! Violet's here!"

She said it like I was expecting Violet.

I got up and went to my bedroom door. I just stood there, and didn't push the button to open it. My hand was on the button, but I didn't push it. I stood by the door.

"Hey!" my mom called. I heard her say, "You can just go up. He's probably asleep."

I pressed the button.

She was coming up the stairs.

She waved, kind of pathetic, like I was going to yell at her.

I just stood by the door to let her in my room.

She didn't come in. She stood just outside the room.

I was just inside.

She said, "Can I come in?"

I let her in. She came in, and I shut the door.

"You didn't give me an answer about this weekend," she said, "but I just figured, I'm going anyway. I don't know how much time I have."

"What?" I said.

"I'm going to the mountains. You can come if you want." She was like, "I'd like it if you'd come."

"When?"

"Now. For the weekend. Didn't you get my message?"

I shook my head. "Oh," I said. "No."

"The other night?"

"I guess not."

"Or the memories?"

I said, "What memories?"

"I sent you all these memories. I sent you hours' worth."

I looked at the rug. I said to her, "No. No, I didn't get anything. Any memories or anything."

She sat down on the bed. "Oh," she said. "Oh, great. So that's going wrong, too. My chat and messaging. I wondered why you didn't say anything. Oh, god. Oh, shit."

I didn't say anything. I just stood there.

She looked up. She told me, "I got here in a taxi."

I went over to my dresser and leaned on it.

She said, "I told my dad I was going to a friend's house. He doesn't know it's you. I figure, what's he going to do? Ground me for the rest of my life? Meaning, like, fifteen minutes?"

She laughed really short and harsh. I didn't think she should joke about that, because you just don't joke about your life. Especially because it can make people really uncomfortable, if you have something wrong with you, and you keep bringing it up in certain ways.

She was like, "Are you coming or not? This is my big time. I'm going to really live." She said, "I'm going to fucking live. I'm going to go up to the mountains and see things, and I'm going to come home on Monday or Tuesday and be like, *I've seen it. I've used every second.* And then each day after that, I'm going to do something different. I don't care. Museums. Shows. Anything."

I said, "I'm kind of busy. I wish I'd got the message."

She stared at me like she couldn't believe me.

I said, "If I'd got it, I could've changed my plans, what I have to do."

"Okay," she said. She was angry. She stood up. She said, "Okay."

"I'm really sorry."

"You don't want to run away together? You don't think that sounds exciting? Better than doing . . . whatever you're doing?"

We were standing there, and Smell Factor was running down the hall behind us, shooting out his broadcast beams *("HEADS UP, TEEN ENFORCERS, 'CAUSE THAT SURE AIN'T THE WELCOME WAGON!")*. Mom was running along the carpet behind him, shouting at him. She slammed some doors. I think she must've caught up to him.

Violet said, "It'll be fun."

She sent me pictures of a cabin with some pine trees, and a fire, and two people with smudged faces that could be her and me sitting there under one comforter.

"Come on," said Violet. "What are you going to do otherwise?"

I didn't want to answer her.

Seriously, she chatted. *What's scheduled?*

I thought about the pictures again, the cabin and the pine trees. I thought about the comforter, and her sitting next to me. I thought about me erasing the copies of her memories.

I said, "Okay."

"You'll go?"

"Okay."

"Oh, this is great. We're going to have a great time."

"Okay."

She said get my clothes, so I did, I took out some clothes and started putting them in a duffel bag. She was all cheerful and kept bouncing herself on the bed and talking about where we were going. She picked up my boxer shorts when I was folding them, and she had this smile, and she put her finger through the vent in the front and twiddled it. It stood up like an elephant's trunk. I watched her. Then she tossed the boxer shorts onto the duffel bag, and I folded them again and put them in.

I told my mom that we were going to a concert and that I was going to stay over at Violet's house afterward, because I thought she would freak if she knew I was going to go off somewhere without having any real plan and spend money on a hotel or cabin. Mom said, *Great, have a good time,* because she was busy running on a treadmill that lit things up while Smell Factor tried to throw marbles at her knees.

Violet and I went out to my upcar and we got in. I asked her whether she shouldn't tell her dad where we were going, and she said no, he was being very protective, and he would birth meg cow if he found out she was gone for the weekend, and with me. I said, *Oh great.* We were flying now, going up the droptube, and I was waiting for her directions. She sent them right to the upcar and it sent confirmation. I could feel it calculating a flight pattern.

I asked her, "So have you been okay?" and she

said, "Things happen—immobility—then a few hours later, it stops, and I can move. I'm worried about the chat, though. That's new. I didn't know. Did you try to send me things?"

I lied to her: "A few things. They were short," but I didn't feel good about it. I said, "You could send the memories to me again."

She looked at me real intense.

She goes, "You can join me. We can prepare. I have this dream that I'll be able to learn to live without the feed. I wish they could just switch it off."

"Can't they?"

"Not dormant. Off. I mean, completely. They can't right now. It replaces too many basic functions. It's tied in to everything." She was looking at the ceiling. "One little thing," she said. "I caved in. The other day, Nina said she'd noticed all of the requiem masses I'd been listening to. She suggested some others. Here's the hideous thing."

"What?"

"I liked them. She figured it out. I've been sketched demographically. They can still predict things I like." She sighed. "They're really close to winning. I'm trying to resist, but they're close to winning."

"Just . . . keep . . ." I didn't know what to say. I said, "Doing."

She looked at me and smiled, and said, "My hero."

I didn't want to be called her hero.

I looked at her, and she was smiling like she was broken.

I reached down, and turned up the fan in the climate control.

It was a college town up in some mountains. The mountainsides were covered with gouges and cables. She had made a reservation at a hotel. It was a cheap hotel, the kind where you always are thinking about urban legends.

We went in to the manager.

"I reserved a room," Violet said.

He said, "Name?" He looked at me.

I guessed, "Mister and Missus Smith."

Violet smiled like we were in a musical and she was about to break out singing.

The guy nodded. He was like, "Yeah. Sure. Smith. I don't give a rat's ass. You're Smith like I'm Betty Grable." He held up a scanner. "Hold out your hands. I'll key you for the room."

I was trying to have fun.

We went out to the room. Violet was like, "What a quaint little place. I didn't know stucco could brown like this." She touched the door, and it opened for her hand. She went in. I went out to the upcar and got our bags. I liked being the man getting the bags. I went in. She was poking around the room. She lifted the covers on the bed and looked at the sheets.

"Check the mattress foundation," she said. "For bodies. They sew them in."

"Okay," I said. "If you dig the pubic lice out of the soaps."

She looked around. "It's the kind of apocryphal story hotel where people usually only stay when their upcar breaks down during a rainstorm."

I said, "Yeah."

She said, "Dead rattlers drying on the shower curtain rod. A man with rulers for hands sitting in the room next door. You know, chihuahuas in the mini-fridge."

We went out to check out the town. There were lights everywhere, and concrete. You could see down off the mountain, all of the lights from the upper layer of suburbs stretching all around for as far as you could see, in loops and half loops from all of the cul-de-sacs. It was cold out, because we were outside on a mountain, and we wore jackets and night goggles. It was the nice kind of cold when someone else's skin, it will be grainy when you touch it. I thought maybe it wouldn't be so bad, being with her.

There was some shouting going on by the college campus. We went into a pizza place and ordered a pizza. We asked the people what it was, and they said it was a protest. We asked for what, and they didn't know. So we ate our pizza there, and got some hot cocoa.

It was good to have the cocoa. I thought maybe some Kahlúa, too, but I figured the only alcohol they'd have at the hotel would be for cleaning tile. I felt like I needed a drink, because I suddenly realized that I was dreading every second.

We got back to the room and touched the door. It was a whole night we had to get through.

She grabbed me when we went through, like it was romantic, and she had the front of my coat in her hands, and she pulled me right up to her and kissed me. She whispered, "I want to experience everything, Titus."

I said, "Oh. Okay."

I hoped she would like get the signal, which was the null signal.

She took off her coat and threw it on a chair. She was going, "I've done some of it before. I had this boyfriend, he played the guitar. Somehow he tricked me into doing a thing or two before I realized his lyrics didn't rhyme." She sat on the bed. She was talking in a way that made me feel like the whole mucusy part of my chest was hardened into a stone and someone threw it off a 0 bridge into a deep, deep hole. "But I've never done the main event," she said. My chest kept on falling, maybe with some ice crystals on it now.

She said, "Sit down next to me."

I sat down next to her.

She put one arm around me. It was kind of awkward, because we were sitting next to one another. She kissed me on the lips, and I started kissing her back. Her one hand was around my neck, and she put her other hand on my leg. I could still feel the most or I guess biggest part of my chest, the lung and mucus part, falling down into the pit, maybe hitting the edge and getting dirty and rolling now, with a kind of squelching noise, and I was thinking forward to when it would be over.

She was kneading me with her hand, and I just sat there. My arms weren't around her anymore, they were back on the bed, holding me up. She was like mushing me up with her hand.

I said, "Ow."

She said, "I really wanted this to happen with you. Right from when we started going out. You're just so beautiful. You lead this life like I've always wanted to—just, everything is normal. We can just be like normal people are, off skiing. We could even rent skis. You know, normal kids, they go off for ski weekends."

I said, "Every year I go skiing with my parents. One year we went to Switzerland."

"Great," she said. "You know the border's closed now, for Americans? Now let's refocus our attention."

I asked, "Have you ever been telemarking?"

She kissed me on the mouth to shut me up. She was holding my hair too, which helped? Then she whispered, "I love you, Titus. This is going to be the most amazing night. This is going to drill eyes in the back of our heads."

She was still working away with her hand, and nothing was really happening, and I tried to move away, and she had her arm around me and was starting to look worried. I felt bad, because it wasn't her fault she was going to die, so I tried to smile, but I couldn't.

She said, "What's going on? What am I doing wrong?"

I said, "Nothing."

She said, "What's happening?"

I said, "Nothing."

She said, "I can tell." She tried again, and even worse, tried to be dirty, like going, "Come on baby, I want to feel you," and all that kind of thing.

Finally, she said, "What's going on?"

I stood up.

She was like, "What's the matter?"

I said, "Let's not."

"What? What's the matter with you?"

I said, "I keep picturing you dead already. It feels . . ." I didn't want to finish the sentence. She was waiting, though, so for some stupid reason, I did finish it, maybe because I was angry, and I said, "It feels like being felt up by a zombie, okay? That's what it feels like."

Her face turned completely white.

I felt like shit.

"All right," she said. "I guess this was a bad idea."

She looked very little, down on the bed.

I felt really bad. I said, "I'm sorry. I'm really sorry. I didn't mean that."

She said, "What did I do wrong?"

"Nothing."

She picked up the edge of the coverlet with her fingers and rubbed it. She dropped it. She was looking what people call "askance." She said, "In tests, they find huge numbers of DNA strands on hotel coverlets."

I stood and waited.

She said, "I went to the moon during spring break to see how people live. When you came along, I thought, 'Now I'll have a boyfriend, like people have boyfriends.' Other people just have fun. They just have fun, and it comes naturally to them. I couldn't believe it when the first

269

night . . . that guy . . ." She whacked the back of her own head. "Like a punishment. The first night. That guy. The hacker. It was like I was being punished for even trying. That . . . he . . ." Now the color was coming back into her face. She said, "Then we were in the hospital. They took me away from the rest of you and told me, 'Your feed is damaged. There's a danger it may be life-threatening.' And I came down, and took you away, and kissed you. And the whole time, I was thinking, *Now I'm living. I have someone with me. I'm not alone. I'm living.*"

"Okay," I said. "Violet, I'm real—I'm real sorry."

"You mean '*sorry.*'" She looked up at me, with her eyebrows weird, and what that kind of "sorry" meant to both of us was that it was over, that I had just broken up with her.

"Yeah," I said. "Sorry in that way."

She thought about it. She said, "I wanted someone to know me. I thought it would be like when you're finally tied to the dock." She thought about it more. She said, "I was brought into the world in a room with no one there but seven machines. We all are. My parents watched through the glass when I was taken out of the amniotic fluid. I came into the world alone." She picked up her shoe and scratched the crust out of the tread. She said, "I didn't want to go out of it alone."

I was like, "That's—see? That's the thing. I can't field this. Okay? You're laying this whole guilt banquet. I can't field any of this."

"I'm sorry," she said, "but I seem to be dying."

"No—I can't field this. You were, the whole time, you were just planning this whole eternal thing, and I was supposed to automatically love you always, but I didn't even know. I was just thinking about going out with you, and we would have some fun for a few months, but to you, I was the normal guy, I was magic Mr. Normal Dumbass, with my dumbass normal friends, and oh! Like the whole, like oh! How delightful, the whole enchanted world of being a stupid shithead who goes dancing and gets laid! You wanted to mingle with the common people. Just latch on to this one dumbass, and make fun of his friends for being stupid, while all the time, having this little wish that you could be like us, without thinking about what we're like, or what our problems are, or that we might not be like saving the environment or anything, but we have our own problems—now you're—you know? You know?"

"No," she said, really soft and angry. "I don't have any idea."

"We've only been going out a couple of months. And I'm supposed to act like we're married. A couple of months. It's not some big

271

eternal thing. We should've broke up weeks ago. I would've, if you hadn't been . . ."

"If I hadn't been what?"

"I didn't sign up to go out with you forever when you're dead. It's been a couple of months. Okay? A couple of months."

There was a silence.

"That's it?" she said.

"Well, it was spring break. That would make it April, May . . ."

"That's not what I mean. I mean, that's *it*?"

"Oh, now you're going to take it all wrong."

"Let's go home."

"What?"

"Take me out to your brand-spanking-new upcar and take me home."

"What's wrong with my upcar?"

"You tell me. You look worried."

"What's wrong with it?"

"The male goat pisses in his own face to attract the female. And she likes it."

"Oh, fuck you. What's that supposed to mean?"

"Do you know what's going on in Central America?"

"Oh, here we—"

"Do you know why the Global Alliance is pointing all the weaponry at their disposal at us? No. Hardly anyone does. Do you know why our skin is falling off? Have you heard that some suburbs have been lost, just, no one knows where they are anymore? No one can find them? No one knows what's happened? Do you know the earth is dead? Almost nothing lives here anymore, except where we plant it? No. No, no, no. We don't know any of that. We have tea parties with our teddies. We go sledding. We enjoy being young. We take what's coming to us. That's our way."

I picked up my duffel bag. "You can finish the like, the sermon in the upcar," I said. "You'll have a couple of hours before we get to your house." I opened the door. "Maybe you can also sing me some death songs."

She grabbed her bag. She explained carefully, "I discover that I hate you."

I said, "Do you want to pay for the room, honey, or should I?"

She realized it had to be paid still, and she said, "Oh, shit."

"Don't worry, darling. I have like all the money in the world."

I paid. I was walking out the door. I felt my credit blotted five hundred and twenty dollars. I went out to the upcar. I opened the door for her. She got in. We put the duffel bags between us.

We flew back. It was night. I had never been someplace with that much of angry in the air, like it was crammed. Like the whole air was buzzing.

Like all of the lights on the dashboard were teasing us. We were hurtling forward, and it was like we were fueled by how much we hated each other.

She was crying. It made her ugly. She crossed her arms on her lap. I thought how ugly she was. Her one hand was limp, like a flipper.

I realized it wasn't working anymore.

I closed my eyes. There was nothing but air in between us. I could say I was sorry. I was almost saying it. We were flying, and I was close to saying it, if only she wouldn't say something sarcastic, something snotty, something about how she had watched us all and tried to be as dumb and fun as us. She looked really alone, sitting there in the seat, with the harness around her, and her crippled flipper-hand cradled between her legs so I wouldn't see it.

I don't know how I spent two hours, it was so awful and boring. I thought about anything else that I could. *You low?* said a banner. *Not for long — not when you find out the savings you can enjoy at Weatherbee & Crotch's Annual Blowout Summer Fashions Sale!* It was a little embarrassing, but I did order a jersey. I did it really careful, in case she was tracking my feed.

The night seemed to go on for hours.

I couldn't believe it when we got to her droptube and went down to the bottom, to her suburb. We flew down her street. There were streets on the ground. They were lit by lights.

At her house, I got out and climbed down. Her father was watching through the window. He would see me and know she was lying about where she had been. He came out of the front door. We were hovering in the driveway. I had gone around to her side and opened her door up, and she was trying to stand. She couldn't get out too good with her arm not working. I held up my hand.

She didn't take it. She wobbled there. She was afraid she would fall.

Her father watched her. He saw what was happening and ran up. He took her hand.

She reached out with her other hand and took her own wrist back from him. She freed her hand from her dad's.

She let herself down to the ground alone, all alone.

She stood between the two of us, looking from one to the other.

I turned around and went back to my side of the upcar. I got in. I left. I flew home.

It was only months later that I realized that the last thing I ever heard her mouth say, the last words she would speak to me, had already been spoken, and they were, "Oh, shit."

So, she messaged me the next day, *I'm not messaging you to say I'm sorry, because I'm not, not for everything.*

But I am messaging you to say that I love you, and that you're completely wrong about me thinking you're stupid. I always thought you could teach me things. I was always waiting. You're not like the others. You say things that no one expects you to. You think you're stupid. You want to be stupid. But you're someone people could learn from.

And I want to talk, if you do.

We both said mean things, dumb things, things we didn't mean. But there's always time to change. There's always time. Until there's not.

That was her message.

I said, "Oh, nothing," when Link looked at me funny. We went out to kick some ass on the basketball court.

summertime

When school ended for the year, Link and Marty and I went to one of the moons of Jupiter to stay with Marty's aunt for a few weeks. It was okay. We had a pretty good time. By that point, I was going out with Quendy, and I kind of missed her. We met other girls on Io, but I was chatting back to Quendy the whole time, even though there were some meg delays in feed service between the planets. I told her how much I missed her.

We had some good parties that summer when we got back to Earth. Marty got a giant Top Quark pool, it was inflatable and huge, and the pool was in Top Quark's belly? It floated above Marty's house. It was pretty funny.

Marty had also gotten a Nike speech tattoo, which was pretty brag. It meant that every sentence, he automatically said "Nike." He paid a lot for it. It was hilarious, because you could hardly understand what he said anymore. It was just, "This fuckin' shit Nike, fuckin', you know, Nike," etc.

Everything was not always going well, because for most people, our hair fell out and we were bald, and we had less and less skin. Then later there was this thing that hit hipsters. People were just stopping in their tracks frozen. At first, people thought it was another virus, and they were looking for groups like the Coalition of Pity, but it turned out that it was something called Nostalgia Feedback. People had been getting nostalgia for fashions that were closer and closer to their own time, until finally people became nostalgic for the moment they were actually living in, and the feedback completely froze them. It happened to Calista and Loga. We were real worried about them for a day or so. We knew they'd be all right, but still, you know. Marty was like, "Holy fuckin' shit, this is so Nike fucked."

The night after I saw them frozen, even though they were okay, I couldn't sleep at all. I kept thinking of Violet and her broken flipper-hand. I kept thinking of her pinching her leg and not being able to feel it. I thought of her lying without moving, but in my thoughts, her eyes were open.

That summer was the summer when all of the bees came out of the walls of those suburbs and went crazy, and people couldn't figure it out at all.

It turned out that my upcar was not the kind of upcar my friends rode in. I don't know why. It had enough room, but for some reason people didn't think of it that way. Sometimes that made me feel kind of tired. It was like I kept buying these things to be cool, but cool was always flying just ahead of me, and I could never exactly catch up to it.

I felt like I'd been running toward it for a long time.

the deep

One night at dinner, when my dad came back from a corporate adventure with his management team, he showed us memories from it. He said it was great and really refreshing, and that it was just the kind of thing to promote team interface, and to get everyone to work out their stop/go hierarchies. They went whale hunting. It was just people and old ships and the whales, and the whales' lamination, which he said was a non-organic covering that made it possible for them to live in the sea.

So he broadcast it to the family. He was all, "Okay, here you see us in the little whaleboat. We've 'put out' from the main ship. We've spotted a whale, and we're rowing out to it. This was awesome. Totally awesome. Can you feel the spray? I loved it. I kept getting it in my eyes and blinking. That's — oh, that's Dave Percolex, V.P. of Client Relations. He's in charge of the bucket of rope. See him waving? Hi, Dave. You can see the head of our Phoenix office there holding the harpoon. So we're rowing out there as fast as possible. It was really rough that day. See, we're all shouting that we need to be going faster. 'Row, row, row!' We have our new intern there pulling at the oars. Hey, Lisa!"

I wasn't very interested, and it was making me a little sick to my stomach, because it was going up and down, and the water was gray everywhere, and so was the sky, and I think Dad must've been sick to his stomach, because the feed was broadcasting his stomach sickness.

"All right. So here you can see us harpooning the whale. Oh, Jesus—here we go! Feel that tug! It's awesome. Totally awesome. Okay, this is what they call a 'Nantucket Sleigh Ride.' You got to be dragged by the whale until it gets tired. Then you can go up to it and puncture its lung. Oh, there: This is later. You can see Jeff Matson stabbing it. He's Chairman of the Board. Wow! Thar she blows, huh?!" There was this big spray of blood.

"How's his wife?" asked Mom.

"Jeff's? She's great, I think. Fine. Okay, so here we've pulled the whale up beside the ship. This was the greatest feeling. Now they have to 'flense' the whale, or remove all its blubber in huge mats. Dude, this is tough work. They have to lift the blubber sheets on hooks and feed it into the 'try-works,' where the blubber, it's all reduced with, you know, fire and heat. It's really hot and difficult, and I felt real bad for the interns you see there doing it, Maggie and Rick. Good kids. Real good kids."

I heard a voice say, *She wanted me to tell you when everything stopped.*

I could barely hear it over the cries on the ship, and the smashing of waves against the carcass of the whale. *She wanted me to tell you when it was over.*

"All right," said my dad. "Here we are drinking a toast. And in the background, you can see — now they get some kind of special oil out of the brain cavity. You have to actually send people into the brain cavity to bail it out with buckets. See? They're dressed up all in rubber. It's an awful job, walking around in the brain. Those are Byp and John, two more of our interns. See John, with the bucket?"

She wanted me to tell you that you don't need to see her if you don't wish to.

I looked for who said it on the ship, because it was a feed noise, but I couldn't turn my head, because it was my dad's head, and his memory, and there was the sea spray. I kept on looking at this like forty-five-year-old V.P. lady and getting completely turned on. I tried to stop looking down her blouse when she stooped down to pick up some kind of flensing spade, and I tried to look for the voice, but I couldn't turn my head, and anyway, it wasn't there with the interns bailing the whale oil, or the seagulls flying over the boat and charging at the slime that was all over the wood.

It was Violet's father's voice.

I am attaching our address, in case you've forgotten it. She told me to tell you when it was all over.

"Never mind the rest," said my dad, and he stopped the broadcast.

"Wait!" I said. They looked at me.

"What was the lady at the end?" said Smell Factor. "She made me funny."

"Yes," said my mom, kind of dangerous sounding. "Who was she?"

"So that was the outing," said my dad.

I was trying to pick up the line from Violet's father. I was searching for it, but I couldn't find it. There was just his message, and the attachment with their address.

I stood up. I said, "I got to go. I just got this message that Violet's . . . I don't know. I think something's really wrong."

My father said, "There's a name we like haven't heard for a while."

My mother said, "Maybe because 'we' have been strutting around on a whaling boat, eyeing up the V.P. of Sales." My mom had lost so much skin you could see her teeth even when her mouth was closed. "What about it, Peg-leg Pete?"

I left and went out to my upcar and got in. I flew out of our bubble and into the main tube, and then out of our neighborhood and up the droptube and then across the surface. People were going by me in streaks of light. The clouds were glowing green, and a black snow was falling.

It was miles and miles away. It was like so far.

On the news, there were underground explosions that no one could explain in New Jersey, and a riot had started a few hours before in a mall in California, and was spreading, with feed coverage of people stampeding for safety and children falling and professional people beating the shit out of each other with chairs and a body floating in a fountain while the Muzak played a waltz.

I had fed Violet's address into the upcar, so it did the driving. I didn't need to do hardly anything. I didn't have the like, you know, the attention, and I wished I didn't have to sit. I wanted to pace until I got there, if there'd been enough room. My legs felt jumpy.

While I got out of my upcar, the front door of the house opened. Her father was there. He left the door opened and went inside. I walked down the driveway. I stood for a minute by the open door. It was dark inside. Then I went in.

There was no one in the living room. There were the stacks of books everywhere, and posters with words on them, and some plants. I called out, "Hello?" and nobody answered me, so I went around the corner to go to Violet's room.

Her father was standing in the kitchen. He was leaned up against the counter. He had on his feed backpack and his special glasses, which were showing him words. He looked up at me quickly when I came in.

I whispered, "What's happened?"

The father pointed down the hall. The hall was dark, with wall-to-wall carpeting that might've had something spilled on it. I went down the hall. I went into the room, and saw her there.

4.6%

I stood there in front of her bed. The bed was floating. She was covered in discs. They were on her face and up her arms. She looked real, real pale. There were signals going on behind her. Beeping and so on.

Her hair had been shaved off, and it was just a fuzz, now. There were scars on her scalp from where they tried to fix her. Her eyes were open.

It was weird to be in the room with her. It was like being in the room with her if she was wood. It didn't feel like you were in the room with anyone. You could stand there and you would feel completely alone, like you were just in a room with a prop. You could watch the prop, and not feel anything, or remember anything about how the prop used to joke with you, and how you wanted to kiss it and feel it up. I had thought it would feel like a tragedy, but it didn't feel like anything at all.

Her father came in and sat down in a chair behind me.

I was still standing up.

He settled in his chair. I could hear his feedpack creaking.

I kept looking at her.

He said, "Her speech became increasingly slurred. Toward the end, she no longer could make the kind of sly witticism of which she was so fond. Your bon mots cannot fly fleetly when each consonant is a labor. She could barely get her tongue to touch her hard palate. She would kick things in anger when she couldn't speak. Until her legs stopped working finally, and didn't start back up again. Then I could see her trapped in there. I could see it in her eyes. For a while. She had also become"—he sighed—"she had become hazy. Confused. The hippocampus was likely being mismanaged, so her memory was dim. She asked me about her mother. She spoke a great deal of you. The worst stage was when one could tell she was still awake and almost alert, but she knew that nothing worked. Imprisoned. She was imprisoned. In a statue like the Sphinx. Looking out from the eyes. Her own mind, at that point, was as small and bewildered as a little fly. Behind great battlements."

I turned around. Words were going across his eyes.

He did not read them.

I whispered, "Oh."

He said, facing toward her feet, "Her mother and I didn't want to get her a feed at all. I did not have one. Neither did her mother. I said none for my family.

"Then one day, when her mother had left, and I needed work, I was at a job interview. I was an excellent candidate. Two men were interviewing me. Talking about this and that. Then they were silent, just looking at me. I grew uncomfortable. Then they began looking at each other, and doing what I might call *smirking*.

"I realized that they had chatted me, and that I had not responded. They found this funny. Risible. That a man would not have a feed. So they were chatting about me in my presence. Teasing me when I could not hear. Free to assess me as they would, right in front of me.

"I did not get the job.

"It was thus that I realized that my daughter would need the feed. She had to live in the world. I asked her if she wanted it. She was a little girl. Of course she said yes. It was installed.

"If they had not installed it . . ." He lifted his hand, and held it, like he was weighing possibilities.

"They say," he told me, "that it was the late installation that made it dangerous. The brain was already wired to operate on its own. The feed installation was nonstandard. They have also told me that if I had bought a better model, perhaps it would have been more adaptable. I remember them asking at the time." He whispered, "I skimped. I read consumer reports and wondered, 'What's the difference?'" He looked at me, and asked, "What could go wrong?"

He was glaring at me.

"I'm sorry," I said.

He asked, "For what?"

"For what I did."

"What about what you didn't do?"

I nodded. "I'm sorry for that, too."

"Sorrow," he said, "comes so cheap."

"You can't blame me."

"Why?"

"I didn't do this."

"You took her to that nightclub."

"She — but she wanted to live. She told me. She told me she wanted to live."

He hissed, pointing at her, "Does this count?"

I looked at her.

She was completely calm. She didn't move. There was a beeping. I remembered her in the hospital on the moon. Laughing. Throwing hypodermic needles at a picture of a man with no skin.

And then he began sending me shots of

memory. I saw her gagging when parts of her throat stopped working. I saw her lying partway on the bed, partway on the floor, tangled in her sheets, her eyes open but not blinking.

I saw her thrashing on the mattress, mooing like a cow for mercy.

I rolled her over with his hands, I rolled her over, and the back of her pajamas were black and wet with her shit. I started to clean her.

I saw her pleading with her eyes. The room smelled like her urine, like something hot and just starting to bud.

I began to cough, and came out of the memories.

He was sitting there, staring at me.

"What a nice visit," he said. "So kind of you to come."

"Stop it," I said.

"You've done your duty. Why don't you go along and play your games?" said her father. "We're the land of youth. The land of opportunity. Go out and take what's yours."

"I'm not a jerk," I said.

"We Americans," he said, "are interested only in the *consumption* of our products. We have no interest in how they were produced, or what happens to them"—he pointed at his daughter—"what happens to them once we discard them, once we throw them away."

"I didn't," I said. "I didn't throw her away."

"And the worst thing," he said, "is that you made her apologize. Toward the end. I didn't say anything to her, but she told me she was apologizing to you for what she said, for how she behaved. You made her apologize for sickness. For her courage. You made her feel sorry for dying."

"I'm sorry."

"You're sorry." He stood up. He was taller than me. Thin, real thin, but tall, with these big, loose hands. He said, "Why don't you go back to your friends, the ones who teased her?"

"They didn't."

"It's almost time for foosball. It will be a gala. Go along, little child. Go back and hang with the eloi."

"What are the eloi?"

"It's a reference," he said, snotty. "It's from *The Time Machine*. H. G. Wells."

I stepped closer to him. "What does it mean?" I asked. "Because I'm sick of—"

"Read it."

"I'm sick of being told I'm stupid."

"So read it, and you'll know."

"Tell me."

"Read it."

"Tell me."

"You can look it up."

"You can tell me."

"Will you ever open your eyes?"

I yelled, "Fuck you! Fuck you! You can fuckin' tell me!"

He grabbed my shirt. I didn't expect that. His big, loose hand was on my shirt. He was yelling like a little kid. He was yelling, "No, fuck you! Fuck you forever and forever and forever! Fuck you forever and ever!" I pushed at his arm. His fingers were wound up in the fabric. He was crying. *"Fuck you forever and ever and ever! Forever and ever!"*

I pushed his arm away. I went for the door.

He was just crying, and saying, "Fuck you forever and ever. Forever and ever."

Before the door shut, I heard him saying to her, "You couldn't hear that, Vi, could you? I'm sorry. I'm sorry. You didn't hear that . . . ?"

I walked so fast I almost ran through the house. I stumbled sometimes. There was a special on draft pants at Multitude. There was a preview of the season opener of *Klang*.

I ran out to the driveway. I went to my upcar.

I didn't fly. I didn't go anywhere. I sat in the upcar. It nudged me and asked me where I wanted to go. I didn't answer. I sat. I sat.

Finally I told it I wanted to go home.

It took me.

Miles of suburban bubbles, the shafts, the

tubes, the pods. Pennants advertising malls. Trailer parks on miles of concrete, with window boxes covered in ash. Upcars flashing past, their prices speaking to me in my head.

At home, I walked around my room.

Out in the hall, I could hear Smell Factor playing action figures. I could hear him make explosions with his mouth.

I sat on my floor.

I tore at my pants. I was trying so hard to get them off that they ripped. I took off my sweatshirt. I threw my boxer shorts against the wall. I was naked. Completely naked.

I sat on the rug. I sat in the middle of the floor. I could smell my own sweat from my folded places. I sat there.

I ordered the draft pants from Multitude. It was a real bargain.

I ordered another pair. I ordered pair after pair. I ordered them all in the same color. They were slate. I was ordering them as quickly as I could. I put in my address again and again. I was shivering with the cold on my butt. My arms were around my legs. I ordered pants after pants. I put tracking orders on them. I tracked each one. I could feel them moving through the system.

Spreading out from me, in the dead of night, I could feel credit deducted, and the warehouse alerted, and packing, I could feel the packing, and the shipment, the distribution, the transition to FedEx, the numbers, each time, the order number, my customer number traded like secret words at a border, and the things all went out, and I could feel them coming to me as the night passed.

I could feel them in orbit.

I could feel them in circulation all around me like blood in my veins.

I had no credit. I had nothing left in my account.

I could feel the pants winging their way toward me through the night.

I stayed up all through the early morning, shivering, ordering, ordering, and was awake at dawn, when I put on clothes, and went up to the surface, and watched the shit-stupid sun rise over the whole shit-stupid world.

4.6%

Two days later, I went to visit her.

I dressed real careful, like for a special occasion. While I was driving there, I kept fiddling with my shirt. I tried the sleeves rolled up and rolled down at different places on my biceps.

When I got to the house, the father opened the door. The father stepped away and let me in. He didn't say anything. He walked into the kitchen and out the back door. I went into Violet's room.

She just lay there. She still had the discs all over her. Someone had laid her arms outside of the sheets. Her eyes were still open.

I sat beside her. I had an hour before I had to go meet Quendy. I put my hands on Violet's arm.

I said, "Violet? You might be able to — maybe you can hear in there," I said. "So I came over to . . . I thought I'd tell you the news, what's going on, just talk to you.

"And I also found some things like you like. The strange facts. About things in other places. I thought you'd like to hear."

I tried to talk just to her. I tried not to listen to the noise on the feed, the girls in wet shirts offering me shampoo. I told her stories. They were only a sentence long, each one of them. That's all I knew how to find. So I told her broken stories. The little pieces of broken stories I could find. I told her what I could.

I told her that the Global Alliance had issued more warnings about the possibility of total war if their demands were not met. I told her that the Emperor Nero, from Rome, had a giant sea built where he could keep sea monsters and have naval battles staged for him. I told her that there had been rioting in malls all over America, and that no one knew why. I told her that the red-suited Santa Claus we know—the regular one?—was popularized by the Coca-Cola Company in the 1930s. I told her that the White House had not confirmed or denied reports that extensive bombing had started in major cities in South America.

I told her, "There's an ancient saying in Japan, that life is like walking from one side of infinite darkness to another, on a bridge of dreams. They say that we're all crossing the bridge of dreams together. That there's nothing more than that. Just us, on the bridge of dreams."

Outside her window, her father was working in the garden. He was on his hands and knees, pulling out pieces of grass from where the flowers were. His feedpack glittered in the sun. I watched him. The sky was blue over him. He patted the dirt with his hands.

And I whispered, "Violet . . . Violet? There's one story I'll keep telling you. I'll keep telling it. You're the story. I don't want you to forget. When you wake up, I want you to remember yourself. I'm going to remember. You're still there, as long as I can remember you. As long as someone knows you. I know you so well, I could drive a simulator. This is the story."

And for the first time, I started crying.

I cried, sitting by her bed, and I told her the story of us. "It's about the feed," I said. "It's about this meg normal guy, who doesn't think about anything until one wacky day, when he meets a dissident with a heart of gold." I said, "Set against the backdrop of America in its final days, it's the high-spirited story of their love together, it's laugh-out-loud funny, really heartwarming, and a visual feast." I picked up her hand and held it to my lips. I whispered to her fingers. "Together, the two crazy kids grow, have madcap escapades, and learn an important lesson about love. They learn to resist the feed. Rated PG-13. For language," I whispered, "and mild sexual situations."

I sat in her room, by her side, and she stared at the ceiling. I held her hand. On a screen, her heart was barely beating.

I could see my face, crying, in her blank eye.

o o o

Feeling blue? Then dress blue! It's the Blue-Jean Warehouse's Final Sales Event! Stock is just flying off the shelves at prices so low you won't believe your feed!

Everything must go!

Everything must go.

Everything must go.

Everything must go.

Everything must go.

Discussion Questions

› *Feed* is set in a future time when most Americans get their news, entertainment, and shopping tips from electronic transmitters implanted into their brains. In what ways are current technologies similar to the feed? How are they different?

› Titus attends School™ but can barely read. What are students taught there? How would these lessons be useful to students?

› What is happening in the world outside the feed? Is it, as the old man on the moon insists, a "time of calamity" (page 38)?

› In *Feed*, product information flows directly, and unceasingly, to the brain. How deeply have commercial messages penetrated your own day-to-day life? Does the presence of that advertising bother you? Are there things about it that you like and that you would miss?

› When Titus and his friends are disconnected from the feed for several days, how do they entertain themselves? What does Violet mean when she wonders: "Maybe these are our salad days" (page 60)? If your life is routinely spent online, what happens when you go offline for an extended period?

› Violet gets very angry and bitter with her new-found friends. Do you agree with all of her accusations about their lifestyle, or do you think she goes too far? For example, Violet complains to Titus, "Because of the feed, we're raising a nation of idiots. Ignorant, self-centered idiots" (page 113). Do you agree?

› "We are a new people," the feed reports (page 149). "It is now the age of oneiric culture, the culture of dreams." What does it mean to live in a culture of dreams? Would you want to?

› *Feed* is always provocative and thoughtful, but it is often very funny, too. What are your favorite comic moments in this novel?

› When Violet is gravely ill, Titus mostly ignores her messages and rejects her pleas. What does Violet need from Titus? Why doesn't he give it to her? Why does she believe he's different from his friends? Is he?

› The word *feed* can be a noun or a verb. Why is it a fitting title when used either way?

On *Feed*

M. T. Anderson

When I wrote *Feed*, my intention wasn't really to predict future tech—but instead, to think about cultural conditions as they already were then.

All around us, ads, TV shows, and movies nudge us with images of the high life, playing on our desire to belong. When I was a teen, this drove me crazy (as it bugs and worries many teens). There's always that subliminal message seducing us and bullying us: *If you just get this, and buy this, and order that, you'll be cool, and you'll be loved. See how much fun these kids are having? If you want to be wanted, then you need to want what other people want. And other people—what they want is this. Buy it. Buy it now.*

This marketing has become even more intense (and not just for teens!) now that most of us are connected all the time through devices of one kind or another. I don't even notice the ads that flit past me anymore, I take them so much for granted. And even though I know that my favorite shows are paid for product placement, I take that for granted, too.

Of course, I wrote *Feed* back in 2001, before most of these devices existed, and before marketing systems had become as sophisticated as they are now. But even then I was still tapped into a wider system of corporate communication. Already my dreams of who I wanted to be, my understanding of who I had been in the past, my hopes for who I'd become in the future—these things had already been influenced and perhaps even constructed by advertising images, movie sequences, and prime-time TV, the hours of images of twenty-somethings crammed into bars, girls smiling at men who drank the right beer, leaving me with a dim impression that I was supposed to like a certain kind of music, a certain kind of shirt, a certain kind of ribs.

So I began to conceive of a story in which these media connections and social networking connections weren't external, but within us all. What if we no longer needed devices? What if we had an Internet feed within us, so we were never disconnected?

It is out of the memory of my anger as a teen at the bullying maneuvers of "youth marketing" that I wrote the book—but also out of the knowledge that even now, I'm part of this system of desire. I still can't get out of my head the images of who I'm supposed to be. (For my current age: the picket fence, the lawn, holding some daughter up toward the sun in a moment of joy about our paint swatches, strapping my tykes into the SUV.)

I don't think this would have been an interesting book to write (or to read) if I had only hated the hyper-marketed world I describe. For me, the key to the discomfort—and the exploration—is how much I love some of it, how much I still do want to be slick like the people on the tube, beautiful, laughing, surrounded by friends. And how much I legitimately do think that the technology-based information resources at our command now are incredible. These are tools for an amazing new understanding of the world, though they come with strings attached. Think about the way technological progress over the last twenty years has revolutionized the artistic possibilities in film or the data-collection processes of medical research—or almost any field. We have at our fingertips knowledge and power like no other generation before us, and that's intoxicating. I am no Luddite. And this would not have been an effective satire, in my opinion, if I hadn't also been seduced by what I was mocking. It is the anguish of indecision that animates it. This is indeed a brave new world, but there is a cost.

My conception of that cost has perhaps changed a little since I wrote the book a decade ago. At the time, I was worried about the cultural effect of this information buzz on how we understood ourselves—even on our own neurological development. Now I am more worried by how this media shell actually *insulates* us from understanding the world around us.

We live in an increasingly complicated world of commerce. It's very hard to track where the things we buy come from, where they're assembled, who's involved in making or growing all of the things we consume. Food is regularly shipped to us across thousands of miles from corporate farms. The gadgetry we love is constructed in residential factories on the other side of the world. Our winter clothes are stitched together in concrete bunkhouses in tropical climes. As time goes on, it becomes harder and harder for any of us to keep track of how things were made and how they got to us. Yet at the same time, whenever we buy something, we're also putting in a "yea" vote for the system that put it together. We're responsible for a world we don't understand.

For democracy to work effectively, there must be an educated and informed electorate. By the same token, for the free market to work, it requires informed and intelligent consumers. We have to comprehend the long-term effects of what we buy, or we are nothing but dupes.

Unfortunately, in a saturated media world, it is hard to find these things out. We are all suspended in a sphere of imagery and voices vying for attention. How do we know that what's going on is actually in our best interest? How can we be sure that our way of life will be preserved for the future? And do we really want it to be?

This is what I worry about now, as I consider the feed and its possibilities.

People have told me that *Feed* is coming true. (Many of the technologies I discussed have been explored in recent years.) But in a sense, I believe it already was the reality when I was writing.

I was already dreaming in advertisements.

New York Times Bestsellers!

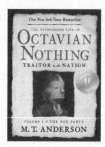

A NATIONAL BOOK AWARD WINNER

A MICHAEL L. PRINTZ HONOR BOOK

*The Astonishing Life of Octavian Nothing,
Traitor to the Nation, Volume I: The Pox Party*

Available in hardcover and paperback and as an e-book

A MICHAEL L. PRINTZ HONOR BOOK

*The Astonishing Life of Octavian Nothing,
Traitor to the Nation, Volume II:
The Kingdom on the Waves*

Available in hardcover and paperback and as an e-book

"Octavian Nothing's story encompasses both the
comic and the tragic with sweeping ambition."
—*New York Times*

www.candlewick.com